THIS NEVER
HAPPENED
SOMEWHERE

This Never Happened Somewhere

Ryan Starbloak

Edited by Melissa Duclos
Cover art by Anna Kira

Visit my website at:
starbloak.com

Also by Ryan Starbloak:

Table of Contents

This one is for Gina & Joe.

Introduction

I said this somewhere in "I Play Pool", the novella that closes "Freckles Over Scars", but it bares repeating: It doesn't matter what you do in life, but who you do it with.

I've been out of high school for six years now, and out of my hometown for over two of those years. As a result, my social circle had really dried up. Enough time pasted of me being single and I resolved that I wanted a relationship. This was something I generally knew about myself at the time and understood why. But there weren't a lot of potential mates in my social life, so like most people in my situation these days, I defaulted to online dating in order to open up some possibilities. And we're all pale imitations on the Internet, I get that, but somehow I'd end up going on a lot of dates with girls whose beliefs system differed from mine. That is to say, they were polyamorous. Don't ask me how I ended up encountering so many of these kinds of people, choosing to go out with them. I might have been curious, or intrigued. But ultimately, as you can imagine, those dates did not go well. We wanted different things, and would sip our ice waters awkwardly as a result.

Right now, I live in New Orleans and am coming to terms with a prevalence of that type of lifestyle here. It's a type of sexual liberation and open-mindedness that I greatly admire.

These encounters form the roots of this story.

It took a lot for me to get here to New Orleans, to leave where I was from (Lynn, Massachusetts). There have been several trips back and forth now, the span of Louisiana to North Carolina in one day then North Carolina to Massachusetts the other. And that's just the pure distance.

Each time, I've traveled alone. It seems to me, the more you do alone, the less hesitation there is to action. Once, I made it all the way back home and my car died a few days after. I turned up with the idea of a road story where a good portion of it was spent *stuck*. Imagine the anguish of ending up stuck somewhere you didn't belong.

As much as I've learned about polyamory and sexuality from people so vastly different from me, I must admit the difficulties I face in taking a stance on any particular lifestyle as optimal or preferred. It's up for the individual to decide what makes them happy. What bothers me though, time and after, is how terrible the average person is at calculating what is best for them. How some people end up dying alone yet some people aren't content even with multiple partners. I can never discount that there are people who polyamory is genuinely right for. What I can do is wonder how we can all find our mates and fulfill our desires in peace.

Another seed of this story which is important to mention is the relationship found in the 2008 Woody Allen film "Vicky Cristina Barcelona" between Juan Antonio, María Elena, and Cristina. Indeed, I know of a couple who felt that a third partner in their relationship would be exactly what they needed instead of repairing existing problems between the two of them.

This story is one I willed forth to expand upon this nagging attempt at a short-term fix for a long-term problem.

You better have a good day,
Ryan Starbloak

"There is no greater healer than unity."
-Reverend Amos Howell

PART ONE: TAMRA

1

I'M HAVING ONE OF THOSE little overtly anxious moments May would accuse me of. It's just me standing still in the crowd and none of them can tell. I could be on fire and some of them might not notice. They are zombies. Okay, not *really*. More like mindless, drunken rabble dipping into a sea of oblivion. The crowd goes in one of two directions: towards Canal or Esplanade, creating confusion.

And if the lights on Bourbon Street go out about now, it would be one of the worst places on the planet to be. It's what I want though, because I know I can just climb up the black fence topped with the row of fleur-de-lis. All the way up to the sign that reads Barter's. For a time, I'd be safe. Panicked fuckers would try and take my spot, but there would only be enough room for me and I could kick them down easily enough. And the thought of kicking anyone pleases me.

Behind me, fueling my desire for the Apocalypse is none other than its harbinger, the song "Watch Me." It's the fourth time the DJ has played it tonight. I try to focus on the synth line, extrapolating that noise from the many other noises further from me, other clubs and their music.

Worst of all, Gary's still meandering behind me on the empty patio of Barter's, dicking around. It's our second night and he doesn't have the hang of his job yet. Not good at all.

I decide I'd kick him down from my spot too.

The breeze from Jean's fan hits me. My throat is hoarse, and it tenses up as I shout: "Yo! Assholes, free round of shots. Make even more bad decisions, and do so at Barter's!" I can pretty much say it how I want. No one is listening. They're a human stream, uninterested in me. There are better

3

things on Bourbon Street to look at than me. Still, I'm staying close to the fleur-de-lis fence to prevent from being grazed, touched, bumped, or groped by the passersby. Most of the people in the crowd are tourists, but there are some homeless mixed in there too. The homeless and I recognize each other; we're both out here all night. The only advantage there is they know I'm not going to give them any money, so they mostly leave me alone. Whenever they do try to hit me up for change, I counter that my money is static. Or sometimes, since they don't understand and their grammar is atrocious, I'll just respond, "I got nothing for you."

Looking over to Jean, I become jealous. Jean the go-go dancer gets more creepers than I did because she is half-naked and gorgeous. She's wearing fish-nets and is twerking. The security guards give her all the attention and make sure she is safe, but as for me, I am on my own out here in the crowd, trying to promote.

Ana, the manager during nightclub hours, knew Hudson when he was here. The lady thought very highly of him. It didn't end well. "Use your flirty voice," she'd told me. "And smile when passing out those cards." Only I don't have a flirty voice, but I didn't bother telling her that. "This street is a bar crawl for bachelor and bachelorette parties and that's who we want the most of in the club, because they are the prettiest kind of people on Bourbon Street. Target them."

Hudson's kryptonite: Those fresh spring frolicking fuckers, almost ready to get married.

Promoting as a job isn't going to get me anywhere, so I'm practicing to be a go-go dancer. There's not a whole lot to it. You have to surrender your body image to the public and be prepared for some handsy weirdos, but the real key is stamina. Jean, minus a few breaks, dances on that little wooden stage 9PM until we closed around 3AM. The rest of it is just shaking with the song. I've confirmed it by watching her, the fan behind her waving around her hair.

Gary is still being a failure. What the fuck, Gary. An empty patio means I have to stand out here even longer. I'll just have to do his job for him.

Mardi Gras is coming up so we figured Barter's was the best way to build up some funds. Gary and I left from Natchitoches, ditching a trailer and video games to make it to New Orleans. We went in for an interview set up through Hudson. Since he'd been their all-star boy in his time, he nearly guaranteed us employment at Barter's. Hudson never did say anything about Jason though. That would have been a nice heads up. We showed up a few days ago and Gary was wearing one of Hudson's brown cardigan sweaters to our interview. It hadn't fit Hudson and it didn't fit Gary, so I don't know why he kept it around.

Jason introduced himself. He was bald and wore thin glasses that pinched each side of his head a little. He looked Spanish to me. Middle-aged. All in all not out of place for a service industry manager. He requested to interview us separately. We didn't like that. Our family is openly co-dependent, but we had to just let it go. For Gary's interview, I stayed within hearing distance along the twisted staircase that led to the second floor. It was my first time at Barter's. I'd heard many stories from Hudson.

When Gary requested a position doing bottle service, Jason chuckled.

"Hudson told me everything I need to know," Gary told him.

"Well, he was a great worker. Are you a great worker? This is a fascinating place. A lot of things come up. All of a sudden, too."

"Yes, Hudson told me."

"What have you done before this, Gary?"

I didn't want to look over to them so I pretended to be playing on my phone.

"Primarily farm work."

"So you've never worked a nightclub before?"

"I can bring in groups. I just need a chance. I will do anything, really. But—"

"We are having issues getting groups in. But there's

something you have to keep in mind: those girls are not for you. Don't touch on them or anything like that."

"Uh, okay. I mean fair enough."

"You start tomorrow!" Jason said with a long nod.

"Right. Cool. Bottle service, right?"

"Yeah, yeah, we'll figure it out. What we really need is someone to be open to do anything."

It was a tightly-vaulted secret that we were only staying through Mardi Gras. So Gary tried to finagle certainty out of Jason that he could immediately start with bottle service. Then it was my turn. I was terrified. Like I said, I was gunning for go-go dancer. I'm not going to rehash the stupid shit Jason said to me. Needless to say, I didn't get what I wanted.

Instead I'm passing out cards to coerce tourists to our bar instead of any of dozens in the immediate vicinity. It'll be my fate until the crowd retreats to their cozy hotel rooms to sleep off the nasty fruit punch mix from their Hand Grenades. What keeps me alert is the hope of seeing a group — five or more girls we could offer a free bottle of vodka and mixers to.

With all of this my anxiety keeps expanding. May told me it's how I function. Bunny had the right figure for go-go dancing, but she'd never be down for it. The opposite of me: wrong figure and into it. Bunny was a princess. The rightful and gentle heiress to a pretty universe that would never be. I miss Bunny most of all and thinking about her just makes me angrier, to the point where anything can set me off. Bunny isn't even far away, but now she's staying in Texas longer than expected.

I flee to the bathroom and brush right past Gary who knows exactly what I'm thinking but not what to do about it. It's not that he doesn't care, he's just numb to emotions. It wasn't any better when I was just May, Gary, and I, but that period of our family certainty held some fond memories.

I head inside to use the bathroom. At least it's starting to empty out. It's getting late and it won't be much longer. Gary had to stay late to close stuff at the bar, but as soon as Barter's closes I am free to go. Problem is that without Gary I would be alone. One of the servers here invited me out for drinks but I can't spare anything on getting fucked-up and I don't want to connect with anyone. No one ever gets us, and people usually end up disliking me when they figured out who I am, so I rather they never know me in the first place.

It seems like my fists are already clenched and my nails digging into my skin before I even get to the ridiculous line to the bathroom. No choice, I have to wait. The employee bathroom upstairs isn't working because Bourbon Street has antiquated pipes and hard water.

"Tamra," Gary says to me loud over the music. "Chill. We are going to be closing up soon."

"I'm fine, Gary. Why don't you go do your fucking job?"

"It is too late. Hudson said that it is improbable to get another group after a certain period of time."

"He also said you have to be tenacious."

"I know but—"

"You're not. So go be."

"You know Tamra, everyone here is treating me like shit. You think you can wait until we are at home to add on to the pile?"

"Now," I insist. I point to the patio. He gets the message and goes back out as the line pushes forward. Eventually I get in there and scream into the cheap paper towels.

When I go back outside I find everyone in the crowd is too drunk. Gary did manage to find another group, but whatever. If I was a boy I'd do it better than even Hudson did. But I'm a girl so I have to do this instead. It is still messed-up they gave Gary a chance with bottle service. Lucky for Gary, he looks like any given blond supporting character in a young adult film adaptation. See Hudson was doing bottle service here for awhile, and he made fucking bank. He wasn't as good-looking as Gary, but he learned how to use his mind to talk to the bachelorette parties. Not without consequences though.

7

My mind speaks up, louder than the music at Barter's. What if this doesn't work and we don't get the hang of it and just keep failing? We'll be stuck in fucking New Orleans! We are literally stranded in this shit-hole on behalf May. Do I even want May? I know I want Bunny. And to a lesser degree Hudson. But May?

If there's anything that gets me angrier, it's the feeling that I actually don't care about gunning for the things I think I want. Because then I'm just pretending to be working towards them, all the while in the back of my head I'm done with it all. I hate how we might not do the things we really want to do. So Barter's needs to appear to be overflowing with women. Maybe Gary sucks at his job but I can still do his and mine, actually pull this off. That motivation comes in waves until I realize I don't know how to find a group either, and then I just don't care about anything until we get to see Bunny again. But that is going to come for sure. I can't wait though. I can't help it. And—

Ah, fuck it. I'm stupid.

I just think of them and our aim whenever it gets too rough. Bunny. Hudson. Then to May.

2

IT SEEMED LIKE I WAS diagnosed with ADHD a week after modern medicine decided it was a thing. So as for my fixation with end days, I grew up exposed to or obsessed with every fictional and possible apocalypse you can imagine. After 9/11, every time a plane flew through our little slice of sky I thought some terrorist was going to crash it and land right on me. I wouldn't pray that the plane didn't crash, instead I prayed that the terrorist nabbed some other little girl in some other neighborhood after mine. I genuinely believed that all future-planning was futile, and as I got older I even got evidence to justify a slump life. Between trickling social security, nuclear arms, and advancing technology making people stupider, it's all a wrap to me. A shitty Hot Pocket I'll scarf down as fast as I can. Yeah, I don't take good care of my body either.

I dropped out of high school in tenth grade and my parents probably stopped loving me. They threatened to kick me out if I didn't get my GED, then they took all their high hopes for me and went all in on my little brother Richard like a bank transfer. God it was like everything I did was about to get me kicked out. But it was my refusal to attend community college that cinched it for me. First the GED, then community college? No. Fuck no. I got the hell out of Lakeland with my ex-boyfriend Travis. The gas tank of his Corolla was never more than half empty and neither were our stomachs, but we always got our hands on whatever drugs our dealer had on sale that week.

Drugs, sales?

Oh wait. I can sling some like before and that's how Gary and I can build up travel funds. Most of the people at

Barter's are already at that game, so it wouldn't be a huge stretch. I think carefully about it, and it itches at me. Tempting me in the middle of the night. But the itching, oh it's real. Shit.

"Mosquitoes?" Gary asks me. "No way." He's mumbling, reaching for a water bottle, having to climb over me. We're renting out a backyard camper.

Things sort of come together in my mind. I seriously hope not but— "Are you thinking bed bugs too?" I ask him.

His plain white tee has two small holes in it, formerly the site of chocolate stains. Gary would rather cut small stains out of his clothes than clean them. "There is no bed. So call them by their real name, cimex lectularius."

We both know he is right, but it still pisses me off. He knew what I meant. This floor isn't *so* bad. "We did not have them in Natchitoches," I say. We wanted cheap housing and we got it, bed bugs included.

"I am going to talk to the landlord tomorrow," Gary tells me. "Try to go back to sleep."

I'm too tired to stay pissy. "I'm not going to sleep. Look, I've got a lot of stuff on my mind."

"That does not makes you thoughtful." Gary chugs his water so he can have an empty bottle to pee in later. "Hudson said he would meet us if we could stop in Knoxville for him."

I saw, in my mind's eye, little bubbles in my heart and fluids fogging up, preparing to boil. Hudson. "That is out of the way."

"I know, Tamra. But what, do you expect him to come to New Orleans then double back up north with us?"

"He could meet us somewhere on the way to Maine," I said. "No, actually, he needs to do that."

"Hudson is shaken up, you know?"

"We're all like that, Gary. He's not currently being eaten alive in a camper with a shoddy roof in an impoverished New Orleans neighborhood, is he? No, I think he's haunting May, cooking his own food, feeling sorry for himself. Too scared to go to May without us, almost too scared to go on those terms anyway. That fucking *bitch*! Let's call him. Right now. I'm not having this."

"Tamra, please relax."

I smack Gary's face, his left cheek. Too bad he has no bites there. Gary hits me back, but not hard. He's just trying to turn me on. "Not now," I say.

"Think for a second, Tamra. Out of everybody, who is still here with you? And you want to fuck *me* up?"

I roll away and walk over to the sink. By the time my cigarette is lit, I'm balling my eyes out. What the hell is he talking about? I don't even care. "Where's Bunny? Why am I here and she's not? Better yet why are you here and not her?"

"We all need to prepare ourselves for what is to come, Tamra. We will all be reunited but it is going to require more from each of us. For me, I have to endure the berating they give me at Barter's. For you, you need to curb your emotions."

"These bed bugs are going to throw us way off course, Gary. We can't fucking stay here. And they're just going to follow us! On our bags, our clothes."

"Then I am glad that Bunny is not with us. Means she does not have to worry about bed-bugs. Then she cannot possibly suffer."

The between of not being with someone you miss and being with them just so they can suffer the same things you are.

"What I don't get about your job is, if *no one* can do it, why do they bitch at you for sucking at it too?"

"Because they can," Gary says.

I let out a trapped batch of air from my lungs. "February 19th in Knoxville. If he's not there we go on without him and he can find himself his own way. Tell Hudson we'll meet him." Gary doesn't know it, but right now he's compromising with me.

"All right, Tamra. That seems reasonable."

Yeah, like I was saying, for my concession, I'm going to

start dealing and not tell him. Then when we have the money while he's dicking around he won't care what I had to do. Things with Gary, well, at this point, I need him to get to May. If it was just May and I here in New Orleans, I don't believe we'd cross the country for Gary.

3

WHEN MAY LEFT US, WE had to let her go. May was actually the worst fucking one out of the five of us. Okay. Wasn't sure how to put that nicely, but I think I did. I might just feel that way because I've known her the longest. Time has a way of ruining people for you. It's like the longer you know someone the less you like them. Another shaky premise for the case of monogamy. How can anyone claim to love someone more today than yesterday? All I get is sick. That's why it was so great with our family. We could spend time with each other alone. Switch off.

We were all living peacefully in Denver and one day she told us about how her mother's condition had worsened, and that her mother didn't want to see her.

"That means, if nothing else," May had said, "I have to go there against her dying wishes."

No one liked the idea. We all sat down and talked it over in a series of pow-wows and meetings, trying to convince May to forget about her mother and let the bitch die alone like she pretended she wanted to. Following so many talks, the matter seemed to have been settled.

Four days later, May left for Maine in the middle of the day when we were all asleep. Families can't stay together forever. One person will move on or get a terminal illness. It was a heinous act on May's part. She *left* us— as in the place where she belonged— to go somewhere she wasn't even welcome.

Naturally things began to collapse from there. We couldn't afford to stay in Denver so Hudson left next, only he said he'd be back. It was ballsy of him to leave, but less ballsy than I thought since I thought he was going after May against our collective decision not to. He went to Indiana or Illinois, in hiding and refusing to step up.

We tried so hard to stay in Denver and have it be just Gary, Bunny, and I. But that shit just didn't work. Bunny just felt left-of-center without Hudson and May, and I didn't blame her. Plus our apartment was being split three ways instead of five. I know I miss Bunny the most. She took a flight straight to Texas because she had family there and knew she'd be able to find work doing phlebotomy. The plan was to follow her but her family just couldn't accommodate two more.

Gary and I ended up in Louisiana so we could at least be close to her. We were just sitting there in a trailer not unlike this Scamper, the two of us snapped inside our own sort of self-contained relationship within the others. That Russian doll within a Russian doll was and still is undoubtedly an unhealthy one, but it was one way to hang onto our family a bit longer.

Gary was doing laborious maintenance and I was some pseudovisor at Payless Superstore. I had gone back on my vow to never live with just a guy again, all in the name of May, who'd abandoned us.

Three months past with no news, no information. Then one day the text came in and in no time we were geared to go, Bourbon bound.

4

ANOTHER NIGHT AT BARTER'S IS beating the shit out of me. The bar manager Cal is bitching at Gary to find another group. It's hard to hear him, though, with Lil' Boosie's "Wipe Me Down" playing.

Gary comes over to me all defeated. I need to help him or he's going to get fired.

"What's the fucking problem, Gary?" I ask. I hear Jingles, one of the homeless people who hangs out at the French Quarter, rocking a cup of change back and forth. There are a lot of regulars in the French Quarter, either homeless, busking, or like me (the worst one to be) employed at one of the clubs.

"Every time I do manage to get a group out here, they kill the bottle and leave!"

"I'm going with Tyler and I'll find a new group. Fix that section up. If it looks like shit people aren't going to think you're worth tipping." I point to the patio where there was a couch and some tables for the promotional bottle service between the two go-go dancer stands.

"Okay. Thank you."

"Bitch, just do it," I hiss. He'll be licking our wounds up later. By which I mean I'll be sitting on his face. He's actually no fool down there, which surprised me considering all his years being fully gay. It's how we've spent the last three months together, but it wasn't enough.

Hudson only told Gary what to do in order to get a group for bottle service, so I'm really just guessing. Bachelorette parties are the best, like Ana told me. And according to Hudson, bachelorette parties had a certain way about them.

A bachelorette party was a group of girl celebrating the passage of one of their own into marriage. Their objective was to have the most memorable time possible. So a lot of them came to Bourbon Street to facilitate this. What was weird about those groups was they adopted a sort of hive mind. They sought out drinks, penis straws, and beads. A lap dance was a must and we offered that service at Barter's.

How we take groups in is we offer them a free bottle of vodka and mixers. Yes, free. Because like the go-go dancers, a group of girls partying outside gives the club some serious visual stimulation and people are more likely to want to come in. They have to be beautiful. So like, not me. Skinny bitches who spend three hours getting ready. That's why we put them on the patio. That's how it was meant to go, but I don't know how to convince a group I'm not trying to hustle them. It does sound suspicious, a free bottle service. I mean it's just well vodka anyway, and Gary runs to get them whatever mixers they want so it's customary to tip.

Hudson told Gary that every bachelorette party he found on Bourbon and invited back to Barter's had the same questions and skepticism. I'm out now with Tyler, one of the security guards at Barter's, and am fucking it all up. Between the promoting and bottle service I know we aren't going to get enough money to get out of New Orleans after Mardi Gras.

It's why I'm with Tyler. I know he has weed. But I want to sell amphetamines. My nerves are getting to me because New Orleans was supposed to get Gary and I to Maine but now it seems to have a hold on us. That, and selling drugs could get me arrested.

Bunny is nowhere to be found and I almost step in a pile of horse shit that's already flattened from all the people walking up and down the street. The shit belongs to a horse from the NOPD: Not Our Problem Dude. They have mounted patrols in the French Quarter. They just let their horses crap and piss and tourists step in it all the time. Sometimes it's funny to see happen but I also have a bit of sympathy for the poor bastards. That's why I always tell people no matter what, never look up when you're on Bourbon Street. Never. No matter how exciting something seems, if you look up, you *will* step in the wrong place.

Group after group declines my offer because they think I'm full of shit. My only satisfaction is some of the girls are wearing heels. Ladies, don't wear heels to Bourbon Street. There are so many different puddles of piss, vomit, and spilled drinks along the curbs and pot-holes. If you do, I'll be laughing at you when fall. It's that simple.

Tyler and I double back to Barter's empty-handed to see Gary out front in the crowd, failing just as hard as me. "Yo, Tyler, I need some moon rocks," I say.

5

MY SEARCH FOR BUYERS TAKES me a few blocks past Barter's up to the darker, sleazier end of Bourbon Street. I'm walking and all of the sudden it's strip clubs and grizzled barkers who look like they've been trying not to sleep for the past week. It's not like the other parts of Bourbon Street are wholesome, it's just the end towards Canal seems to harbor even more broken dreams and bloody noses.

I'm meeting up with some friends I met who live in the apartment by the Scamper Gary and I are renting. Their names are Livi and Thom, and they are into what I'm into. So naturally they want to help me in exchange for some of the moon rocks I've obtained. Today is just a test run, so I'd left most of the moon rocks in Gary's black backpack.

To dull my edges, I drink some Evan Williams, sharing the handle with the two of them once we find each other in the crowd. There's a constant rattling noise from foot traffic over a loose grate that led to a deep hole in the ground. I wish it would collapse on them. Livi and Thom were humble people. They have their shit together and will probably even have a planned baby someday.

I don't really understand babies. It's something I get hung up on with those conventional couples. After they've been together for long enough, it's like a baby is the next assumed step. Like, society's always pushing people to make these few distinctive choices and make them seem desirable and logical. And I don't know—people like Livi and Thom should be coming up with plans independent of societal norms, but it's obvious they're not. Makes me uneasy, since Livi vacuums up cocaine from Mexico with both nostrils. That shit is no good. I tried some to make sure.

We stand outside of one of the many strip clubs nearby, The Hidey Hole. It's Thursday night and it's late so there's some debauchery on the street. Mardi Gras is just around the corner and it's showing as more tourist unload their pent-up nonsense. Gary better not cross me about selling drugs. Livi goes in by herself while Thom and I wait with the bouncer. He looks like all bouncers always do: short hair, bad posture, and facial hair on his chin and upper lip.

"What's it like out here?" Thom asks, looking up to the bouncer. Thom never comes out this way. No reason to, given Livi.

"I'll tell ya," the bouncer responds, roused from a statuesque daze. "It's no good tonight."

"What about most nights?" I ask.

"I don't know. It's the same really. Bourbon Street's the place where it's okay to be naked but for the wrong reasons."

"Why's it no good tonight in particular?" Thom wonders.

"One of our female barkers no-showed so the only incentive for anyone to come in is my ugly mug."

"Do you like it other times at all?" I ask him.

"I get tipped-out, 'cause I help clean."

"Yeah, I kind of get why your chick didn't come out. I'm a barker up the street, but it sucks rotting dick."

"That right?" He looks at me, sort of lighting up. "Where at?"

"Barter's."

"We need a new female barker really bad. Not to strip, just to dress skimpy, stand outside, and entice the guys to walk in. I think you'd be great. You've got a nice body."

"Really?"

"Yes. Are you interested?"

"Only if I'm making more money," I say.

"Certainly. Go inside and fill out an application, talk to my manager. Here's the thing though. See, I might be out here with you, but do you have balls? You got to have balls."

"Oh, I've got balls."

"I'm serious."

"Tamra, are you really feeling this?" Thom asks.

I nod and walk in, and Thom follows. We cross paths with Livi, who informs me that her stripper friend is interested. "Only twenty-five is too high, Tamra. She likes to haggle."

"Motherfucker." I am so bad with my money. I own that.

Peering at some tits, I try to stay focused on my way to the back. There are some private booths and mirrors on the walls. A saddle-door leads to a room with a desk. This man in a suit hands me an application. For a strip club. This is hilarious.

It gets less comedic when I make it home. Gary isn't happy. I debate telling him I made some sales, but eh. "Two jobs, Tamra? You are somehow late to Barter's half the time as it is," he points out.

"That's why I'm fucking quitting. If Bunny ever makes it out here, she can have my spot."

"Bunny will not want to work on Bourbon Street! She is going to stay in Texas until we are ready so she can make the most amount of money. That is how this can happen."

"I need her here ASAP."

"Out of the question. We need to get to May. Maybe we should extend our stay, Tamra."

Blacking-out is something I've never done. Just tiny little moments of disconnection, little rage episodes. When I'm angry I visualize, like that boiling blood. Then comes a desire to murder everyone in the immediate vicinity. Totally feeling it now.

Bunny wasn't here, so I suppress myself somehow and tell him, "No."

"We might not have a choice, you understand that, right?"

"No."

I don't listen to him anymore and when I do open my ears for his rationalizations, he's not even in the Scamper. I don't care.

I absolutely cannot tolerate living with just one guy, one

person. It's like we're Livi and Thom at this point, and that's fucking untenable. After seven years with Travis I swore I'd never live with another guy again. It also swore me off monogamy. Seven years of paranoia and shit was enough.

That's what we're programmed to want, a partner, a lifetime experience with someone. Well, someone's always an asshole, and if it's somehow miraculously not you then it's your partner.

My time with Travis was turbulent, but that doesn't mean it wasn't meaningful. I was in love. Deep love. I'm sure because he was perpetually bad in bed. I cooked him dinner once when we only had enough food for one.

That last tidbit has to do with my body image, which is fucking nothing I care about these days, but somehow life fattened me up to a point I never bounced back from.

From Lakeland, Travis and I went to Atlanta. Living out of a car with no income got old after a month, but we didn't have enough to get out of there. It was what we'd always dreamed of. We were so moronic.

The city was so unlike Lakeland or anything else I'd ever experienced before. I can't forget the smell of the dumpster we lived across from. A year-and-a-half went by until I actually admitted that I wanted to go home. Travis thought I meant him and kept fucking me.

We had some miscommunications. You know, home is where your heart is but a vagina isn't such a bad place to stay if you're a dick. It didn't matter if I was on my period— he fancied having streaks, consecutive days of sex. I just gave up on stopping him at some point there.

We scraped by in Atlanta doing random shit like waiting tables or working at AutoZone. It was just us, as far as we knew. And we were paranoid. Travis thought I was fucking people and I thought the same of him. See, even if he was, I was stuck with him. I knew I hadn't cheated on that fucker yet. Which is not to say I didn't do worse things.

One night I got kidney stones. It was the worst fucking agony I've ever had to go through and it got so bad that he actually stopped having sex with me. Yet the guy was bitching that I had kidney stones. Enough was enough. I forced him to take me back to Lakeland so my parents could bail me out.

The look on their faces. That smug satisfaction. The feigned acceptance and forgiveness of my sins.

It was freaky being back home and it would have been best to break-up with Travis, but he was my only way back out of Lakeland. We headed out as soon as it was possible. And it was possible because Travis was peddling cocaine. There was a descent as I tried cocaine for the first time. It was ruthless stuff, but not as bad as the Mexican brand I would try later from Livi. I don't even trust drinking those Mexican Cokes.

The cocaine didn't help our relationship, but we did manage to get an apartment in Myrtle Beach. I had nowhere else to go. My parents wanted the best for me, but I had no idea what that was. What mattered to me was being out in the world, playing *Left For Dead*, and volunteering at animal shelters.

It was at this point that I did sleep with someone else: a girl. I can't explain it but she looked just like May, except she wasn't May. Not then.

6

"HEYA GARY," I SAY AS he steps through the door of the Scamper.

"I was just talking to Hudson."

"I remember him."

"Yeah, he wants to talk to you." Gary hands me the phone that I didn't realize he was holding.

"What's up, motherfucking bitch?" I ask into the phone.

"Tamra, I believe in what you're doing. I'm sorry I'm fucking up and not showing that," Hudson tells me in his trademark quiet tone.

"Nice."

"Look, on your days off now, go to Barter's and deal. There's plenty of clientele there still. The DJ with the afro huffs whippets. He should still be working there, I bet you he does."

"Hold on, how did you know I was uh," I look over to Gary. Then I remember I stuck some moon rocks in his black back-pack. And he was holding the moon rocks. Butt-fuck it.

I talk a little while longer to Hudson than I otherwise would have because I'm dreading the confrontation with Gary. I actually listen to Hudson for once. Then Hudson hangs up and Gary starts right up.

"Hey, if you are going to sell these, fucking sell them. Do not make me carry them around. You are out of your mind!"

"I'm so tired of you. This is supposed to be a team effort!"

"It is, and we each agreed selling drugs would be more of a liability than anything else," Gary points out. He throws his back-pack on the ground, surrendering it to the bed bugs.

I go over and get the moon rocks— still not a hot ticket item — and split to try and peddle some more. The goal is to sell the rest of them (twenty-three to go) before we leave.

Before I make it out of the Scamper though, Gary starts yelling again. Usually I go on the defensive when this happens, but this time I just cry and take him into my arms. My empathy is rare, and I think it was Bunny who first brought it out of me. Because I'm enraged, I just know I need Gary.

A few hours later, Bunny calls me.

"Come to the front of the house. I'm here."

"Wha...?" I ask and realize. Surprise, surprise. Just when things seemed their darkest, Bunny pulls one over on me. She's in New Orleans. I almost bash Gary's head open trying to get up. We're scrambling for clothes to make it out to see her. Running from the side of the house to the front porch, I can't believe she's really here.

"Bunny!" I shout. She's just standing there, looking cute as ever in a prude dress and black stockings, with a red clip parting one side of her hair. She's half-Korean, half-American and so short. And she is here.

"Why didn't you tell us?" Gary asks her. We haven't had a moment like this since we got the text that liberated us from Natchitoches.

"She needed this," says Bunny. "And so do I."

7

IT'S THE END OF GARY'S and Bunny's shifts and Ana hands Gary one hundred sixty-eight dollars. I don't like Ana, but I get how Hudson did. He'd still fall on his sword for her.

"This is from the free ones outside tonight," she says to Gary.

"Nice work," adds Cal.

I myself made forty dollars and I had to haggle to be rid of the moon rocks, but the buyer also gave me some weed.

We walk in the aftermath of another weekend night on Bourbon, the street littered with garbage, still a few drunken morons gallivanting around, experiencing the decrescendo of the passed-out district. It's cold out in the gray light and I see Hudson's cardigan that Gary is wearing has a purpose for once. He wasn't happy about Bunny leaving her steady phlebotomy job for Barter's and neither is she. I seem to be the only one who is happy. Well, not happy. You never want be happy. It's too much to have taken away.

"How'd you pull off those tips, Gary?" Bunny asks him. It's less than what Hudson made on a normal day, but far more than what Gary had been managing.

"I pretended to be sweet, timid Hudson. I tried to talk like he would talk. I repressed my assoholism. I was just *there* for those girls."

"I noticed that," Bunny says. "They loved you a lot tonight. And you were amping them up even more with those bubbles and sparklers."

"I was there with what they needed before they needed it."

"Which is what Hudson said from the start," I say. I'm a

little buzzed because I had the night off from my job at the strip club, but I still gave Gary a hand. More than he'd do for me when I was mostly nude outside the strip club. But that didn't matter. We were finally making headway. Fucking finally. Soon we'd be on the road and Bunny would be present to diffuse Gary's bullshit.

Jingles is doing his thing as we turn the corner on St. Louis.

"Should we go for the Volvo?" Bunny asks me.

"No, you're only on a recon mission. A better deal could spring up if we're patient."

Bunny goes straight to see the guy selling it. I figure she must be tired of staying at this CouchSurfing host's house. She can't stay with us since we are itchy as shit still and are troubleshooting what the fuck to do about the bed-bugs. The landlord isn't going to kick us out, but he's been giving us limited support. So Bunny is temporarily staying with some someone didn't like, because he's a guy. Which means unless he's gay, that he opened his house up to traveling girls most likely to score with them. Bunny isn't going to have that so it's going to be awkward for her. Never mind that she's weary of strangers as it is. CouchSurfing is not an activity for her, but she's sucking it up to save on living costs and thus get us the fuck out of NOLA. I attempted to show her how to accentuate her Lolita style for dudes to eat up, dolling up her femininity. That way they'd try to keep her around as long as possible. Luckily, the CouchSurfing host did turn out to be gay and willing to let her stick around at least until the week of Mardi Gras, which isn't really much longer. We are barely going to make it. It's like we figured shit out just in time.

Still though, we're lost as to what to do about these bed bugs short of wrecking what little we'd saved up on an exterminator. Instead we keep scratching and not sleeping, waking up in the middle of the night *knowing* they're there, sucking us down. But they're so damn hard to find, I don't know why I even bother trying. Bunny is safe though, because we're refusing to hug her until this mess was over.

So in a way we have solidarity. We just have to make it through the main event, the most chaotic New Orleans happening every year— Mardi Gras. It will be a challenge. Since it'll be so busy on Bourbon, we'll make more money than usual, but at the cost of our sanity. It'll be a seven to ten day marathon of fifteen hour shifts. And I know we are all for it.

"I love us all," I tell them as we part for the night.

"And also I love us all, too," Gary says in a monotone voice. Then Bunny kisses me. I can still hear Jingles. There may be a rhythm to his tune, but it's hard to say.

8

I TOLD TRAVIS STRAIGHT UP that I'd met this girl at a college campus and he didn't seem that upset. She came over the next time and he wanted to have a threesome. He wasn't discrete. The girl who wasn't May yet said something like fuck that and left.

I didn't like any of that. My relationship with Travis just plain opened up. I was fed up with one guy for so long. I wanted to experience other things. It was an exaggerated desire for that discomfort I sought out over the traditions my parents upheld.

They were such an effective, functioning team it was impossible to ever divide them. Everything they hit me with was a joint effort, premeditated. They were married for seventeen years by the time I left home. I don't know if they were happy with each other, but I do know they will never get a divorce. It was irksome to grow up like that and think that's what I wanted, because I was told to. I was told I was going to be married and it was going to be great and I'd be treated like a princess. Instead I was scooping cum out of my vagina most of the time because Travis preferred to cum inside of me. Got to make the other person happy, give them what they want. So maybe after they would give you what you wanted.

But it was also opened up because I just couldn't leave him. We started fucking so many other people we couldn't even live together. Eventually we transitioned from lovers to fuckers, and then it was simple to cut him out of my fucking regiment. The girl who wasn't May graduated from college.

That's about the time she became May, and our relationship became official. Travis fought to get me back, but all that did was solidify my vow never to get stuck with a guy alone again. Yet here I am.

Gary stumbles in and walks over to me slowly. I smell his body odor. His hair is a mess, fluffy receding tufts. "Tamra, I almost got shot."

"What?" I hop out of my chair and look him over. He is fine.

"Just now, on Dauphine and Conti."

"Did they get the stuff?" I shake him. He was already shaking on his own though.

"Fucking dick-head points a gun at me and runs off with the back-pack."

"With the shit?" I ask him. "How could you lose the moon rocks!?" Then I realize he has his back-pack slung around his shoulders.

"Yeah, fucking nice cop intercepted him. Got the bag back. Way to keep your shit in my bag. If the cops had looked that over, I would be done for. Next time move them when I ask you."

"Gary, we can't leave it lying around here. The door barely closes. And it's really our bag now." I said that because we are just going to have to throw it away anyway because of the bed-bugs. So why not make it a free-for-all?

"Nope. Your responsibility, Tamra."

"Yeah. That's what you'll be saying about me feeding you when you're out of money."

"Hey, if this is our bag, then whatever we all make is our money," Gary says.

The entire encounter forces me into taking one of the moon rocks. And they're weak so I take another.

9

THERE'S ONE LAST ORDEAL WE have to pull off before we go and that was Mardi Gras. We take all the available shifts that we could, me even taking some hours at Barter's in addition to The Hidey Hole to the point of ridiculousness. At Hudson's suggestion we set up a temporary living space on the roof of Barter's using our hammocks and a rain tarp. Ana is okay with it, but I can tell Cal is a little weirded out. Thing is, Ana and Cal were sleeping at Barter's all week too, on a cot stuffed up in the attic.

Ana's here telling us how much she misses Hudson and I guess I do too.

"Yeah, he really is something," Gary tells her. I can tell he's resentful. We just focus on setting up the hammocks. This arrangement works out well, because we can abandon the Scamper early and save on rent, as well as isolating ourselves from those fucking bed bugs. The worst part is probably getting undressed and having the bites flare up again. I was about ready to start fucking sleeping outside. So now I am. Above all, it will help us get into the mindset of camping. When we finish we have a tiny hut of empty boxes we use to help block the wind. It isn't that cold, but it's still February. This will test our mettle. We all lie down in our separate hammocks to test things out.

"Bunny, we never talked about what happened," I say from my hammock. She didn't get the text, only me. We all wondered why that was.

I can't see Bunny, only the black fabric of my hammock. I hear her say, "It doesn't matter. I'm okay, Tamra. We're all going to be good. I've settled for the truth."

Gary asks, "How long will it take to get to Maine, do you think?"

"If we don't stop we could be there in thirty hours."

"We have to stop for Hudson," says Bunny.

"Oh right," I say.

"Other than that, are we going non-stop?" Gary asks.

"We have an obligation to get there as soon as possible, Gary."

"It's going to be unlikely we will be able to do one straight shot, Tamra," Bunny argues. "We're going to be cramped and exhausted. I think we should all decide here and now not to lose our cool when it takes a few days to travel to the other side of the country."

"I know, Bunny. But May's—"

"You keep getting ahead of yourself," Gary says. "Hudson first."

"He's not putting us first."

They don't say anything back to that. Bunny starts humming some music. I can't tell what it is.

I fall asleep. When I wake up, I commit to selling the rest of the moon rocks at some of the clubs on Bourbon, but fuck it up and take more. Then I walk up and down Bourbon Street and stare at all the licentious regulars. There are people painted in gold, blue, and silver. Statues. Impoverished black dudes singing shit from the 1930s. People frozen in time. There is Jedi Master Noodles, who offers light-saber lesson dressed up like a Jedi. And of course there are the Bible Soldiers, those protesters of drunken reverie on Bourbon Street recite angry Bible verses and call for fire, discomfort, and lukewarm water in Hell. I can't believe it, but most of these French Quarter regulars pass me up on thee moon rocks. I tried them all. Except the Bible Soldiers. I hate them. They make me want to rip the megaphones off their necks and yell, "JESUS, save us. Save us your followers." For a long time these ignorant cracker-munchers stood tall with a giant wooden cross, passing out propaganda pamphlets, uncontested. Recently though, I've been noticing a few awesome people standing a few paces away from them, spouting rationality and philosophy against the dog-shit-ma with their own megaphones. Sometimes I talked to them about how we, even the most intelligent of us, shouldn't expect to be logical all the time. That we should account for moments of emotional inhibitions and work them into our morality. Not excuses to be rude or ignorant, just concessions for human nature. Scrapping perfection, in other words. A new morality: try not to be a dick.

But tonight the philosophers aren't protesting so instead of having a restored faith in humanity, I take another moon-rock, little capsules of brown crystalline wonder, before this Mardi Gras shit goes all out. My being is a chemical fire.

10

IT'S MY EYES THAT FEEL the worst. All of the horror and exhaustion seems to be seeping through everything I could see. The pressure to get out of this hammock and start another day hits me. It's get up, work, collapse, then do it all over. Maybe some food makes its way in between if we are lucky. All I remember from last night is finally being done and next thing I know, the DJ's music played, booming loudly through the walls and ceiling to wake us this new morning. Our ear plugs are useless. This was not our greatest idea. The three of us moan nonsensical syllables to one another in delirious jolts until we are as good as unconscious again. On top of that it is actually kind of cold for to be sleeping outside. But then once more, it's time to start up another day. Whether we slept only three hours or not.

Gary has it the worst since he was bar-backing and trying to maintain the groups of girls on the patio outside. It's two jobs, and Bunny and I tried to offer him relief without missing out on what we had to do.

My little trip the other day made me feel worse than Gary seemed. Each day of Mardi Gras that goes by unhinges us all a little bit more. Sink showers are all we have, but I'm used to those. It's time for me to get to The Hidey Hole. I give Bunny a hug and then they're on their own. Everyone shows signs of fatigue, even the drunken masses. Small personal cracks. Ana and the other ladies I work with apply glitter under their eyes to cleverly hide the bags. I wasn't going to bother with that.

Tits, all these tits make me think of May's tits. May's tits were the tits. It was a very tender set-up between the two of us. There was nothing her boobs couldn't do when I held them. We had both known the burn of a bad relationship so we found time for each other, refugees. Travis was old news as May and I tried to find her a teaching job. You ever move to a new city and act like an exile from your old one? It was like that when May and I left Myrtle Beach for Raleigh.

Every third step on Bourbon Street is beads. The people are flashing their stuff. It's disgusting, gratuitous. But this is the best way I know how to make money. These tourists come from all over the world to see boobs being flashed or to flash their own boobs. I just don't get it and I don't want to understand anyone who does.

Mardi Gras is traditionally done in conjunction with the Catholic period of Lent. A believer chooses something to abstain from for the entire period of Lent. So before the abstinence, the whole of New Orleans goes wild for a week so they can essentially make up for lost time during the upcoming Lent, rendering the whole premise obsolete to me. And don't even get started on the fact that most of the people partying at Mardi Gras aren't even Catholic.

Ew, there are ugly tits everywhere. You're going to need some whip cream for those tits. It's weird to think our time here is almost up. That things are coming into place with all this in the background.

One of the people bumps into me, walking his bike. "Fuck you with your own bike," I say.

He's one of those guys who dresses up in drag and just stands around. He apologizes. I don't give a shit.

I walk over to the Hidey Hole and pull dudes into the strip club. It's a lot like any other job, except I have a spray bottle of bleach in my bra if someone starts asking for it.

11

FOR AWHILE WHEN I WAS a teenager, my parents had me in therapy for rebellious and malicious activities. I was angry at the world and the world was indifferent. I liked my therapist so much that I played mind games with her. It was weird because one day she asked me what my end game with Travis was.

I told her I was going to love him as long as he'd let me. And I'd never be deceitful to him no matter what. And that was for an asshole.

We're driving north and everything is going great. Money is tight and it feels like gas has already absorbed half of what we made down there in New Orleans, but it was about what we wanted the amount to be with a little extra since Gary really got the hang of bottle service at the end. He suggested we stay another month to secure a foothold, but we had the car, a shitty but functional Chrysler. So I demanded we leave the day after we were recovered from Mardi Gras, as planned.

"But the situation has changed, Tamra. We need to account for it," Gary told me. "Is Maine really so urgent?"

"No, fuck off. I don't think anything's changed."

"Tamra, you're just freaking fight with everyone over semantics," Bunny said. Bunny almost swearing is a big deal. Trust me.

Anyway, I got my way in that we left for New Orleans just as we had planned, but the concession is we are still arguing. Twenty minutes ago we crossed the Tennessee border.

"You know, it really is not all about you," Gary says.

"Serious, you're really self-centered and won't listen to reason," Bunny adds.

I didn't have to listen to reason. "I don't get this. Just let it go. We're well on our way."

"We should just stop somewhere in between after Hudson and post up a few weeks and get another job," Bunny says.

"No!" I object.

"Why not, Tamra?" Gary asks.

"I cheated on us! On all of us. In Denver," I admit, finally.

Not even four hours later, the Chrysler actually dies on us. I heard the signs from the engine, but I knew there was nothing I could do about it on these roads set against miles of an entire country. As we take in the fact that we're stranded, I think my confession weighs on Gary and Bunny even heavier.

PART TWO:
GARY

12

NO ONE UNDERSTOOD WHAT WE were, and I found that odd as it was not that complicated. Maybe there was not a word for what the five of us were that resonated with them, because we considered ourselves family. Family is powerful, and it is not something that is created exclusively by giving birth or having the same grandparents. A sense of family is a very common phenomenon, but given a few conditions it can be rendered as meaningless. As meaningless as some people thought the five of us were together. Our family.

For instance, think of all the people switched at birth by accident. Those parents believe that that is their child, and vice versa. That relationship is contrived. A mimicking of an actual blood relationship where there is not one.

No, family is not what people think it is. There is nothing especially holy about a nuclear family. Why is it so important to most people in the world considering how simple it is to knock someone up? My family looks out for me more than they would anyone exactly like me because well, they know me. Yet if I chose not to communicate with the people who raised me, they would probably be hurt. But see I need to question this idea of the intrinsic value of family because everyone knocks the value of ours. To us, it is just love. Incest is impossible, but Bunny is still as off-limits as if she were my seven year-old daughter. We understand that.

Another thing about our family is how it became so contradictory to my own life and beliefs. I am more gay than straight, but living with Tamra for these last few months has been fine. There has been almost no urge for a guy in my life, except for Hudson. It was a strange but comforting shift.

Three years of being nothing but gay to fucking Tamra and May casually.

That was a different time, and maybe our family was not meant to be understood by others. Those inside are the ones who need to understand; the rest were irrelevant. Our relationship has gone through many different stages and even been defined differently each step of the way as Hudson and Bunny came into the fold.

Our family has separated, but Tamra cheated on us back when we were still one. Each of us had to deal with it in different ways, as in on our own. And that seems to be the largest misconception with polyamorous relationships. Our relationship was still closed, goddammit.

We are six days out of New Orleans on some quaint plot of American land. The Chrysler was damaged fucking goods. Tamra was able to tell because her ex-boyfriends showed her everything she needed to know about the anatomy of an engine.

"It was running bone dry," she shows us. "Engine seizure."

The question of what now bounces around in my head. There is no way we are going to be able to get another vehicle, but Tamra does not seem phased. We sold it for scrap parts.

Why she failed to check over the Chrysler when it was apparently dying is something I am still not getting, but I decide not to fight with her. It is not the time. There is March in a northward direction to contend with, nothing but our hammocks and make-shift tarps.

Tamra's been isolating herself as we walk in Hudson's general direction, states away. "We should keep the faith," she says.

"Half ass-hole half atheist," I grumble. "All Tamra."

Not long after we are waiting at a Subway for a pick-up truck that arrives and pulls over. Tamra starts talking to them and then three bicycles are dismounted from the truck-bed.

"I found these on Craigslist," says Tamra. "A kind of

home pawn shop. They even agreed to meet us."

"We're going to bike to Maine?" Bunny asks.

"What the fuck, Tamra?" I add.

"They were a hundred dollars. I'll take it out of my money." None of us have our own money. She was not getting that.

"Let's just re-configure our meet with Hudson and go from there," she says. "We're stopping in Harrisonburg."

"You. Really? Suggesting we bike hundreds of miles in the winter? Tamra!" I check my watch to confirm. We've missed our rendezvous with Hudson. I can see him, standing in a light pile of snow, shivering, thinking something about us, something awful. And personal. That he should have never left his house that day or any other day so from now on. Yep, that's Hudson.

"The end of winter," Tamra corrects me. "I'm going to pedal this guy until I can't take it anymore, then I'm going to pedal more. You guys are actually right, but for me there's no turning back and we have a long way to go. Stay here if you want." She starts biking away. "May needs us."

Bunny and I actually make it on those bike with our packs. Poor girl was wearing her blue dress. I only feel sorry for Bunny, that girl is not made for travel. I do not even think she knows how ride a bike.

13

BIKING GETS OLD ABOUT TWO hours in. Quelled by sweat that remains on us in ridiculously cold crevasses, I try to ignore the sensation. I still have some bug bites and have no idea if we really had rid ourselves of the bed bugs or if they were some stragglers with a knack for survival slowing us down. That is another thing I am afraid to ask Tamra. Something about actually going through with biking up the country-side has changed her.

Everything natural seems to resist our journey to May, only we fight against it, our supposedly unnatural relationship against the elements, parasites, the car, the wind. Our satanic relationship.

Yeah, right. Most mammals are polygamous, humans are one of the only exceptions. I blame agriculture and religion. Now here we are thousands of years later thinking it's how we are supposed to be. All those fucking movies and love stories. Skinny bitches and lovable losers. Breeders. If modern man had any idea where it had come from, it would put marriage down like the sick dog it is. Current moral trends are not supportive to lengthy contracts like that. Secular ethics is slowly trickling through our culture, but still people have these dumb-ass desires to be loved, forever, by one person. That is a rarity at best. People ought to wise up.

Surprisingly, Hudson agreed to meet us farther south than Knoxville. In a few days, if we could keep our pace of twenty-eight miles a day. Every burn and sore inside of me I blame on Tamra. Then I feel more for Hudson, May, and Bunny being cheated on than I do for myself. All this strife we have to go through together. As if *we* were the ones who cheated.

This is why I wanted to wait in New Orleans just a bit longer. My knees are still aching from all that bar-backing at Barter's, over a hundred hours during that last week leading into Mardi Gras.

What I know of the beginning of our family was from May. She was a sentimental one. Sometimes Tamra felt like a wild animal who did not even have memories or a conscience. She has such an *I win, you lose* attitude but it is not like I am unable to see what May saw in Tamra that foggy morning when they met. They told me they were jogging.

We stop for the night to camp in some woods off the road, so exhausted we go straight to bed without dinner. We all just silently fall into slumber next to each other, hoping the rain would not fall tonight because we had not bothered with the tarps.

As I drift into a peaceful state, I am hindered by the fact that Tamra broke the rules. Whether we were in a monogamous relationship or a polyamorous one does not matter. I want to try and understand why she broke the rules we had all set up, but I am afraid to hear the truth, which is what she would give me. Tamra only lies to herself.

14

HERE IS SOMETHING JACK KEROUAC never felt like mentioning: waiting for the next toilet you can take a shit in, but uncontrollable twitches inevitably forcing you into the forest when that toilet fails to come up along the open road. I feel pity for the girls, because I can feel their discontent. It is unnecessary for them to tell me their pain. They might not know that I notice, but I do. I really try to hold this bowel movement until we met up with Hudson at the next McDonald's, but that is out of the question.

Later, when we reach the McDonald's, Tamra, Bunny, and I are changing clothes outside in the parking lot, sorting through our things. Some of my stuff is in Bunny's bag and there is no hope of reorganizing each other's things into our own packs.

I see that fucker and it makes me bump my elbow off of a guardrail as I start to get up to greet him. I wonder if it is the flannel of his I have on which is causing me to scratch above the sore spot on my elbow or if it was some stray bed bug clinging to life.

"Behold, it is you," I say. Hudson looks fine, not like us (Bunny and Tamra have abstained from make-up at this point). His skinny jeans make me aroused but his lame black skull cap brings me back to normal. On top of that he decided to bring his pea-coat that was too big for him.

Hudson is smiling as we all come in for a hug. This guy has a lot to account for, and I know I will be on edge until he pays up.

We go into McDonald's and split the Chicken McNuggets order four ways. Five nuggets per person. I have a reality check and know Hudson is still a wimp, so I go in for the kill. "Did you leave to go after May and then chicken out?"

"I don't know," Hudson says. I hate it when he does that. He is so uncertain about everything. From how he was feeling or if he was hungry or which Matthew McConaughey movie he thought was stupid, it was always, "I don't know."

But you know, I can always count on his uncertainty. It does have a tendency to allow me to make decisions for him. And at this point, as long as decisions are being made, it does not matter to me.

"Re-phrasing the same question," Tamra says, "What were you doing back in Indiana?"

"I needed some me-time," Hudson says. This is the first time I have heard of him needing alone time. My skepticism overpowers even the need to itch my arm.

By the end of those McNuggets, Hudson has been integrated back into the family, if he ever left it at all.

"I saw my family and some old friends but mostly I did keep to myself," Hudson speaks up after we tell him about the travails of New Orleans.

"That's a long time for you. You faced winter in the north. You told us you would lose your mind if you ever had to go through that again," Bunny says.

"I might have."

"I wonder how close you got to going to May before you chickened the fuck out," Tamra says.

"That's already happened, Tamra," says Bunny, dabbing her cheeks with a napkin. "We don't have to blame one and other for our mistakes. We can set our sights on what's next."

"I'm glad you're thinking that way, Bunny. I have a map here." She takes it out like it was a secret, a trump card and a distinction, a higher devotion to May. "I'm thinking we get a rental car like we talked about. But you know, actually do it now that Hudson's here. Otherwise, he needs a bike and we lose time."

Tamra flip-flopping makes me wonder why she wasted

money on bikes in the first place. We made it a good ways considering, and we still can, so I say so. "Let's at least get to Harrisonburg. Stay there for a night or two. We will be able to rest and go on bikes at least until Pennsylvania to get the rental car. It is a serious bitch biking Hudson, but Harrisonburg is not really that far off. We can play pioneers." I feel amazing. This was an adventure, an end upon itself. Constant reminders of what is at stake, a capricious breeze that could slow us down or speed us up. The world as an obstacle, not a spectacle you saw on television. Roughing it. Arguing. This is the life.

Even so, our plundered, pedaling legs are nothing compared to the real pioneers, crossing the seas starving and sickly, leaving a home to make a new one. The four of us are so safe and sheltered. There are no bad-asses anymore. Not relative to the colonization of American at least. People cannot even conceive of the torture every day brought. We have blenders, they had cholera.

I snap out of it and the conversation has carried on. "We'll need to stay off of the highway," says Tamra. "The police have already bugged us. Fuck, Hudson, they think we're time travelers or something."

"Then we know what we're doing then," says Bunny.

"Mmm," I say.

For the rest of the day I focus on Hudson's skinny jeans and it makes me think of jacking him off and wanting to be jacked. It would just feel so right. Instead I settle for coercing Tamra to do it later, then me jumping it. That would be how it usually got done.

15

IT TOOK A YEAR FOR Tamra and May to get sick of each other. They were in love but too honest with one and other. Fact was, they could not sustain a healthy relationship without some dick. As much as they just wanted it to be them, they really did not. As sick of guys as they were, they knew it was a necessary evil. And that would be where I came in, which like I said was odd because they must have had so many other options. But they chose me.

I was in Winston-Salem, North Carolina while they were living in Raleigh. Our social circles collided one night at a bar and they wanted *me*. The guy who thought maybe eighty percent of his sexual was homosexual. Periods aside, I just find it easier, and I am one for simplicity.

Yet something about their offer intrigued me. They recruited me as a provisional penis, so I could still have flings with other people and they could contact me when I was needed. It was a great deal, and eventually I just ended up leaning on them for sex. Like I said, simplicity. At one point, when I was really starting to get to know the two of them, I inevitably asked, "Why me?"

Tamra did not have an answer, so she made some bullshit up. But May knew and she elaborated: "It's because I've determined you can handle it without being a dick. See Gary, you have a dick, but you aren't a dick." After that, I started going over their place for things other than sex.

I reluctantly accepted their offer to be in their relationship, which became our relationship, actually surrendering during the negotiations to be only with them. Being with just Tamra and May was an aberration in my life, begging the question of what my gayness was. Was it they were gay and they were so awesome with each other? Or maybe it meant sexuality and gender were irrelevant when the people are special enough to you.

For awhile I really didn't mind that much. Gay porn filled in the gaps and for awhile we were great. It was a wonderful thing until I realized I had fallen in love with the two of them. I am certain we became somewhat confused as to how the love was supposed to be distributed, but we did our best. Before Tamra and May, I mostly just sought out twinks to devour. Those urges came back to me, same as Tamra and May's urge for a man came back to them. See, we understood one and other. Even so, I started feeling guilty when those pangs for a flat chest and rough hands started surfacing. I did not belong with them, but I loved them. They told me from the start to always be honest with them, so I told them. Well, inferred. It was May who stepped up and told me, "We have a glorious thing, we do. And it can only get better from here. That's why I propose we open up our relationship one more time. But not just for us. It's time to save someone. A lonely boy. They're all online. Boys who, in their eyes you can see the remnants of all the porn they've been watching. Someone who is open-minded, love-sick, lost. Let's find him and love him."

Tamra and I agreed with May. It did not mean that we loved one another less. We all needed another guy to balance things out, because none of us wanted to leave one another. We just thought we needed balance.

16

"IF SOME ASSHOLE ADDS ONE more post to post-postmodernism, I'm going to learn how to have a mental breakdown and aim for faces," Tamra says.

"Yeah, when was pre-modernism? It's so relative," Bunny adds.

"Exactly," Hudson says.

These truckers are listening into our conversation behind us. I can tell because they stopped talking to each about *Die Hard*. But I'm okay with them listening, as long as they do not figure out what we are. Like I can usually tell by someone's accent if they will or will not accept us.

We move on then take a break in the woods.

It should be raining, so I dance. But it is cold enough that it could actually be snow. The only good thing is that the bed bugs are definitely gone. At least for me, who knew about Tamra. I really wish I would save my energy, as we are starting to climb in elevation adjacent to the Appalachian Trail, full of savory wanderlusts trying to open their minds to the truth, discontent with wherever they have come from. Some of them are even ready to dismiss the experience itself as truthful. Maybe the four of us should be turning back away from May, hiking all the way back the way we came. To run away from what we are going to.

"You're so out there, Gary," Hudson says with his wet shaggy hair that I want to yank. "Take it down a notch." Yep, yank it down.

"Dance with me!" I demand of him.

Tamra and Bunny rest up against a big rock. Bunny takes a picture with her phone. That is her thing, documenting each event as opposed to being a part of it.

As for Tamra, she is not meant to dance. "You're going to tire yourself out and bitch tomorrow morning," she goes. It was funny seeing as she is the one who is calling out all of the breaks.

We continue until six and Tamra wants to stop for the night. It is miserable, soggy enough for that to happen without any contention, but in the back of my mind I am sensing our proximity to Harrisonburg like no one else is. The land is starting to take on a familiar shape, so that while there is a sameness to every road we have traveled down thus far, I feel like these are ones I have seen before. Our collective stamina is depleting. At first twelve hours of biking a day was a fair thing to shoot for, now it was beyond comprehension. Biking across the country is not hard, even when considering the fatigue that was my spirit and the soreness that was my crouch. It is more a matter of impractical velocity. May gets brought up now and then. All we can do at our slow pace is know we are getting closer to her.

Every time we stop it feels like we lose half of a day. But when one of us decides the day is over it is pretty much unanimous, and with the snow still falling from the sky our first priority is to set up a fire. I nibble on a banana between gathering handfuls of tinder when we settled on a small clearing surrounded by skinny trees under a bed of soft moss were the brittle branches had all fallen in numbers so high that every step we took snapped the pieces apart. We try to isolate the gray wood. Thankfully, I liberated a few trash bags from Walmart so we could have some protection against the melting snow. I might have purchased them, but we only needed four and we could not afford to be wasteful. I was the only one spunky enough among us to steal. I think Tamra said she used to do it, but now she is grown up. She can cheat, but stealing is unthinkable.

I get the fire going while she watches me. I would have thought she would just shut the fuck up for once and help, but no. She has become insufferable, even calling dibs on the purple bike when it came off of the pick-up truck. It had skinny wheels so she knew it had to be the fastest. Once the fire is going, Hudson and Tamra walk off. I guess not everyone agrees with my sentiment regarding Tamra.

It is just Bunny and I for the first time in a long time, like one of those rare days back in Denver when our days off exclusively coincided with one and other.

"They have got to be fucking," I say.

"Yes they do. It must have been awhile for him."

"Been seeing them both warm back up to each other. Tamra was into it but she was still evasive to him. Her period is on its way out and so we have this."

"Hudson wasn't even there when she admitted to cheating in Denver."

"Yeah, but I made sure he knew." I groan, then rubbed my stomach.

"Do you want trail mix or actually venture into the minestrone?" she asks me.

"Minestrone, but we will be sure to save some trail mix for the hopping horny hedonist and her thrall." My words come out and the cold air irks my teeth. I move closer to the fire. "Bunny, how was Texas?"

She curls her shoulders upward in a gesture of ambivalence. Then something comes to her. "I was safe but alone. Well, I had my family, you know. But I was still alone. I'd rather be whatever I am now. And yet it's silly, isn't it? Feelings of safety and security? It's so silly. How we go to school for something we've imagined wanting to be."

"Nah, I am sure Texas beats this. I know you were comfortable out there."

"Drawing blood. Whatever. That's not what I want to be. I guess it's just fair for what I make."

"Oh, Bunny. You were unhappy?"

"I was. Not anymore."

We cook the soup and finish it quickly, but we could have taken our time. Tamra and Hudson miss out on our effort this way. I take Bunny into my lap and we lie against each other, letting the fire die. They could worry about it when they got back.

Bunny is so tiny and light in my arms, sometimes I do think of her like a daughter. Hudson does not. Screw Hudson. Hiding and waiting while we took care of the hard parts. To think I surrendered my say on Hudson's induction into the family. May had a way of making decisions for you, just like I do with Hudson now. She had a tendency to word things the way Tamra and I wanted to hear them.

The three of us made a dating profile on Okcupid.com, posting a picture from a dinner date where we were all dressed up nice. We did not put any bullshit up, only that we were looking for a single bisexual male to meet-up with and possibly include in our relationship. We wanted to say family, but thought it might confuse people.

We searched and did some waiting. The horrible messages we got back were indicative of society's ignorance of what a polyamorous relationship is. Our objective was another partner, not to jerk-off a stranger. There was a lot of messages directed at me, personal nods from dudes, none of which I liked, commending me for my prowess in having two girlfriends.

It lasted for about two months but we remained together and patient. I forget who found Hudson, only that it was not me. We brought him out after talking to him for a week or so, going to a concert in Raleigh where we all lived at that point. He was in between places visiting.

I thought he was cute, as did Tamra, but Hudson did not really captivate May. We asked him what he liked doing and he told us he was not sure. Only that he traveled around a lot. He would just go from one place to the other, being broke, then saving up and going to another city and being broke again.

"Why?" May had asked him.

The explanation he gave was one of the demonstrations of confidence I have seen from Hudson. "I need belonging. Where I'm from I had none. So I would rather elect to be alone in a new place on the off chance that the vibrations are just right for me. I thought it was New Orleans for awhile, but I left there with more questions than answers."

Even though he seemed great, we were nervous. He was asking a ton of questions about us to the point where we realized he had no experience in anything polyamorous.

When he was nearly disqualified, May appealed to us. May, the one who was least captivated by him. "If he's willing to give it a try, let's let him."

Tamra objected and I was on her side. Hudson was conventional, plain, reactive. "You have to think," I told May. "Most likely he is going to hurt all three of us for giving him a chance."

"Let's just keep seeing him if he wants to see us and see where it goes from there guys," May said following a contemplative silence.

A few weeks later, the four of us woke up together in bed. Hudson and I were as far apart as we could be with Tamra and May curled in the middle.

I tried to remember how we had fallen asleep, if we had been closer. I have no idea still.

17

A NOISE THAT HAS BEEN persisting through my unconscious state wakes me up. We have not gotten much sleep, but I do see Tamra and Hudson are set up in the double-sized hammock. We all snap up then freeze as a series of howls roll through the wind. The wolves seem nearby, menacing. I am terrified and I still cannot move. The others are whispering to one an other about what to do, but we all stay still. Too frightened to move, too jolted to fall back asleep.

"We can't be attacked by wolves now," says Tamra.

Gradually, and I would not be able to say how long after the howls occur, we set up the fire again, the only thing we have that might stave off the wolves. There is no way to know how much danger we are in, so our minds simply assume the worst.

Out here in the wilderness, the only sign of civilization is a vacant road some yards away. None of our cell phones are turned on because we had stopped paying the bills in order to save money. We have no idea where we are anyway.

"I can't sleep outside like this anymore," Bunny says.

"I know exactly what you mean, Bunny," Hudson adds.

"Guys, we're all afraid right now. So can it," Tamra says.

"We could climb the trees if we hear them get any closer."

"They may be able to sneak up on us though," Bunny suggests.

"Just fucking maintain the fire, guys. We probably have nothing to worry about," I reason. "But fuck it, you know?"

The conversation shifts from a stuttering terror to anything we can think up that would send our minds away from panic.

We end up on nudity. It all stemmed from May, because most of the time she would not take off her top when we were having sex. It bothered Hudson a lot, but Tamra and I just accepted it. Then there was Bunnny, who I have never seen naked.

"See, why does anyone have to feel bad or ashamed about their body?" Hudson wonders. "It's just a body, we all have them. Parts, natural things on us. We can try to alter them but for the most part we are what we are and each of us needs to do our best to take care of what we have."

"It's the things we can't change, Hudson," says Bunny.

"But we all have that in common."

"Some more than others," says Tamra.

"Still. If we're all in agreement, why not just cancel it out in favor of being concerned about more important things?"

"I like where you are going with that Hudson," I say. "It would be tough, but I think the world has to collectively find a way to frame nudity in a non-sexual way. In other parts of the world guys are wearing skirts and women walk around all day without tops on. No one gives a shit or thinks twice about it there."

"Meanwhile, we grow up here in the states and it's like, you must conceal yourself," says Bunny. "Your body is a disgrace. Or it's disgraceful to 'show-off' your body."

"Ah, Bunny, these guys have no idea what goes on when you're a girl," says Tamra. "It's so much worse. We're raised to hide our bodies in fear of being raped. That if we show too much of ourselves, we're inviting that. It's awful."

"Well fine," says Hudson. "We should just all be able to walk around naked if we want."

"Out of shape people like me would never go for it. Also, I don't think you're listening to me."

"Yeah," I say. "So Hudson, what about your parents? Can they walk around naked?" I smirk, knowing his argument is squashed. The wolves are still in the back of our minds but we regard the damage society has wrought as more urgent. "I say some people need to have clothes on. Like your parents, Hudson. Like people with irredeemably small penises. Now, they can do whatever they want in the privacy of their own homes. Just in public, no way."

"But you are sexualizing nudity then," Bunny says.

"And who cares if a penis is tiny?" Hudson asks.

Tamra looks at me and we crack up.

"Oh, you guys. You know what I'm trying to say."

"Yes, we do," Tamra says.

"And it," I say, "is damn near the stupidest, most hilarious thing I have ever heard you say."

"Now Bunny, even if we, here, decide to stop sexualizing nudity most people are not going to change their views."

"It's a start," says Hudson. "If people only realized there was a time when there was no such thing as clothes. Man. Like, we didn't invent clothing to save us feelings of being ashamed. We invented clothes to help us survive in the harsh elements."

"You know for men it used to be taboo to be shirtless on beaches? Like it is now for women?" asks Bunny. "Enough guys just kept pushing and the cops eventually let it go."

"Now women are doing that and people are just taking it as a joke," says Tamra.

"So it's really about gender inequality?" says Hudson.

"Yeah," says Tamra. "And if guys like you, guys like Gary, and even guys not like you can just finally say, hey women have had it bad enough over the centuries, it's time to let that go and all be people, we may have a chance."

"A chance to lounge around in public without clothes?" I ask.

"A chance to save on laundry," jokes Tamra.

When our nudity discussion ends, following a long silence accompanied by a gray light passing over the sky, and a new morning grants us a feeling of safety from the wolves, she goes, "What are we going to do if we get to Maine?"

18

AFTER THE HOWLING FIASCO IN the woods, we decided to get to Harrisonburg as quickly as possible for the purposes of shelter. I am not looking forward to it, not like the rest of them. They are much more traumatized by the wolves than me, and also there are no painful memories for them to recall in Harrisonburg, unlike me. I know I am going to have to power through. For May.

When I was younger, the doctors told my parents I was pretty much retarded. The specifics of it are hazy but needless to say they were wrong. I had a learning disability to overcome. My father used to take me hunting, he would go for the deer and leave me to figure out the snares without showing me what to do.

"Use your instincts, you little turd!" he yelled at me on a particularly turbulent weekend out in the forests beyond Memphis. "This human race has foraged for food and survived centuries long without knowing how. That's the meaning of instinct." My dad was not a huge fan of evolutionary theory.

In a way I have a lot to be thankful for from my father. If he had not been so domineering, I might not have realized I was gay. His own friction opened my mind. Still, try being gay in Bartlett, Tennessee. Our family lived ten minutes away from the Bellevue Baptist Church, the largest mother-fucking place of worship in all of Memphis.

It's like there is no preparing a parent for when their children disappoints them. It is probably just part of what parents are. Just like children are bound to disappoint their parents. Parents should be taught to get ready and deal with it so when it happens they can react reasonably. Then again, there are a few common sense things. Like if you do not want your kids to smoke, you need to, need to quit. You think you can smoke around a kid without consequence? And I am not talking about secondhand smoke. Now, if you are totally cool with your kid smoking, do whatever you want. Otherwise, do not think you can hide it. It is not going to work and you're going to look like the biggest leaky asshole when you try to lay down the law.

They both pushed me into the Navy and I did that for a little while, going to classified places on a submarine. That did not very last long. I did not belong there and those military officer fags will throw you under the bus every time to save themselves. I received a dishonorable discharge, ranking out as an E-3 (a promotion I may or may have not received performing fellatio on one of those aforementioned officer fags).

I crashed in Winston-Salem, North Carolina with an old friend from Bartlett, a girl. When I heard she had an air conditioner, I knew I was in the right place.

Winston-Salem offered more options for a gay guy than Bartlett did. But the time spent there was not about me, it was about the girl. She was convinced she had been possessed by a demon that her mother had exorcised out of her, only a residual primal evil remained in her spirit. One time she came at me with a knife. I wanted to visit her as we passed the latitude of North Carolina, but it was just too much of a detour.

Instead, we reach Harrisonburg, turning the corner of our bikes onto W. Water Street, and I see them sitting under a dying porch light. My parents three years after my dishonorable discharge.

It looks as if they have not moved a single itch since then.

19

FOR BUNNY, HUDSON, AND TAMRA, staying at my parent's relocated home in Harrisonburg, Virginia is rejuvenating. They sleep on the dusty pull-out couch in the basement. My mother is making them home-made banana bread, indeed treating them with all the honors and privileges reserved for guests in her home, all the while she fucking *hates* them. Not as much as she hates me though. It feels like I am diverting some of her hate for them. If it were just me gunning for May, I might have passed up my parent's house entirely.

"What are you even doing?" she asked me earlier today. "It's been three days. You're stalling, Gary. You know you're all crazy going north in this weather. I won't let you stay here much longer."

"I never asked that of you," I told her, turning away from her and looking out of the side window of her Escalade.

When we pulled up the dirt road to the house we saw Bunny and Tamra giving each other an Eskimo kiss on the front lawn.

"What is that, what is that?!" my mother wanted to know. She threw her arm out of the car towards the girls and they missed it entirely.

"Bunny. Like the animal. She loves pretending to be an animal," I explain. Bunny rolled around like a dog. Sometimes she even licked her wrists like a cat.

"That's something children do."

"It sure is," I said, satisfied with the statement. She had a very vague understanding of what we were. Honestly it was just better that she thought of me as gay, so I never updated her.

Things got worse when Hudson accepted some timid sniffs from Bunny. He reciprocated. I wanted some of that.

I saw our family cat, Cheetah, presiding over the porch indifferent to what disgusted my mother so. We got him when I was eleven, before the onslaught of my gayness came over me and my parents stopped wanting to know what I should name our pets. Cheetah was still kicking, even with some cancerous growth that made petting her smoke-gray fur a bumpy venture. When they fixed her my younger-self felt it was such an imposition against nature. I still rile at the phrase *fixed*. As if functional genitalia is broken. The term should be reversed to make sense, but I guess no one would want to "break their cat." Is it ethical to fix a cat because it is unable to conceive of the idea that it can no longer produce offspring? Are we as humans just trying to convenience ourselves by saying too many cats would be an impediment on our own lives? It comes to me because there are more arguments for why people should be fixed than animals. I want condoms air-dropped over middle schools. There needs to be some serious change with society's attitude towards unwanted pregnancy. It is not that hard to have sex without impregnating someone. Just follow a few simple rules and you will be all set!

So many people really should not exist. They should have been blow-jobs. But no, people wanted to go all the way and cum inside with reckless abandon. That's what I think of when I see all the people that are complete fuck-ups, assholics, and criminals. Why they are not any good at living their lives. They should have been swallowed. Yes, that is what they were meant to be. Instead we have terrorists and Mitt Romney. All of whom could just as easily been cum shots to the face, wiped up, tossed out, and no longer a possibility.

20

I DESCEND THE STEPS TO the basement, eager to finish our load. We have to move on. The four of us have cut down our wardrobes so much that we could do laundry in one load. Transferring our contents from the washer to the dryer makes me feel like it's the first time I am seeing Bunny's undergarments, pink panties with Hello Kitty on them. Then there was Hudson's usual briefs, the same ones he had in Denver that could usually be found on the floor of our bedroom.

For awhile we were convinced that it was going to be just the four of us, with some small concessions for open side affairs provided the correct procedures were followed. It was more of a theoretical system than an actualized one. So I never got why Hudson started criticizing it.

"If we're all happy and in love, isn't it wrong for us move outside of the relationship as they please?" he wondered.

"No," I objected. "Not if we are all in agreement. If it even ever did come up. I am telling you, it never does. But Tamra, May, and I do not want to be in a relationship where we suddenly find ourselves wanting to hook up with another person but are unable. It is savagery to hold someone up like that, we all agreed on it."

"I never did."

"No. I realize that now."

"What about loyalty?" Hudson continued.

"Love isn't a fucking currency, Hudson," Tamra said. "It's like having another child. You don't run out of love just because you already love your first born."

"What she means is, it doesn't have to be that way," said May. "If you're unhappy with how things are set up, to be honest, tough shit. This is what we opened up to you."

"You had no one." Oh Tamra, so vicious.

"It feels like I still don't if this is how it works around here. I just don't understand."

"But we understand what you don't," said May. "If you let us explain—" That's about when Tamra and I stopped listening to May. She was always really defensive of Hudson. Giving him the benefit of the doubt. Saying he needs us more than we need him.

I started to regard Hudson's taste in men as a hoax. May wanted me to give him time. Now there was a currency for you. All time gave us was a new city. Hudson suggested New Orleans, wanting to give it a second try. Until we all went to New Orleans, Hudson had not been living with us.

We were all happy enough in the Big Easy. At least between the times we were on the streets. It was just two weeks, but it was nasty. Nothing was missing in our relationship, but that did not mean we could not accept more love. Or did it? The ambiguous nature of the closing of our relationship seemed to be an ideological regression of what May, Tamra, and I stood for. But we each loved Hudson so badly that we let him have his way. That form, that path had but one vindication: Bunny.

The four of us would leave tomorrow morning so I packed away our clothes.

When I go upstairs to brush my teeth, the final night at my parent's house down, my father comes up to me. Skipping over all the pretense, "Are you sleeping with all of them?"

"Yeah, sure, whatever," I go. And I just know I could not have said it any better than that.

"I'm not gonna judge you, but that's no permanent lifestyle though. Next time I see you, you'd better not be homeless."

"I'll keep that in mind, dad." Yeah, not seeing him again that is.

21

REREADING MAY'S LAST TEXT WAS pointless. The first time was enough. If I thought seeing my parents was bad, it is nothing compared to what is ahead.

Tamra saw me, and she sent an oblivious Hudson to kiss me on the lips. We are in the middle of the city square and he picks now to be affectionate?

"You can stop faking it now, Hudson," I tell him.

"You're just paranoid. All the time with this, Gary. You suck up all the attention. Dancing around, yelling when you're drunk."

"You cry when you are drunk like every time. What do you think garners more attention? Yelling does more good than crying any day."

"Well you're right as always, eh dude?" First his gaze trails away from me, then his feet turn away from me. Perching himself against the fence of the baseball field, looking away from me, he says, "Negative attention is all I ever bring to myself when I talk, so I've learned to shut up. But you, you're like Broadway-quality. It's all positive energy and everyone wants to be around you and you're chill."

"Learning to shut up was a stupid lesson, then," I say. "Gratitude, not attitude, is what my mother told me growing up." Positivity. His scarf is off-center, so I close in on him and adjust it.

At first he resists me, but he lets it happen. "Thanks."

"See, I am not sure why it matters to you anymore. We are family. Screw my parents, come to think of it. Maybe they took us in and fed us, but they are miserable and want me to go kill Middle Easterners. That is not who I am. Keep being who you are, Hudson."

He hugs me and we make-out. It would seem like he missed the point, but I relish his scruffy face, brushing my cheeks against his.

Our joints and muscles were feeling drained back out on the road, and I think of how that was probably the last time I will see Cheetah ever again. That house was not the one I grew up in, but it had things from the Bartlett house, making it look like a bad trace job. What was good about back then was not knowing I would be here now. Thinking I would have a career in the Navy like my father tried to program into me.

Free will is so cool, even if it is nonexistent.

As Hudson continues kissing me, I remember those nights in Denver. Vanilla scented candles blazing, lighting up parts of our bodies. Often times, I am hesitant to embellish the sexual facets of our family, because most people I talk to about it associate it with fruitless promiscuity, an animalistic frenzy. But have you ever heard of an orgy and wonder who those people are? See, that was not us. We were in love. If we were that orgy, we would not be here now, sacrificing ourselves for one of our own.

Indisputably the most challenging part was getting everyone comfortable on the bed. Once that was taken care of everything else went fine. I would be on top, driving myself into Hudson while he had just enough pivot motion to both plow into May and meet his mouth with May's mouth beside Tamra's pussy to lick it. There was nothing sexier. Usually, I just jerk myself off while being fucked in the ass or vice versa. But with the girls there too, Hudson could both penetrate and be penetrated. The experience was rare indeed. Hudson would exit May for Tamra, her tongue licking up both the residue of Hudson's saliva and Tamra's juices. And to Tamra the switch was incredibly arousing. Even on a bad day Tamra would come if they did the switch on her.

I do not believe polygamous relationships deserve to become the dominant manifestation of love in the world.

Sexual liberation. It is not some new solution to ancient problems, but it would be nice for people to detach themselves from those sickening stigmas. It is an individual's choice, and people need to be able to make informed decisions. Humans are animals. Societies are man-made. Our true nature deserves as much attention as our societal natures. I know of people who condemn it indefinitely just because they think it is weird. It is not weird and it is not gross to have and share multiple lovers. It makes me think of how life began, the reproduction aspect of it though. Probably there was a distinct pile of cells on top of each other like us, and boom! There's the next thing. Or like this: it is probably how life propagated following its initial inception. One became two became four became eight...

Think about it. Little bacteria cells splitting off into different, identical parts. A multicelluar organism. Seeing piles and layers of single cellular orgasms in a primordial pool of creation, what is so off from May, Tamra, Hudson, and I on top of one another, feeling up where it amps up the dopamine and oxytocin in our heads, building into a euphoric rapture coinciding with a trust in these people so deep and final that our lives are bound together. The truth: maybe, just maybe we were a little co-dependent back then. But that sex was so fulfilling! So much pleasure and care.

While all of this was going on, Bunny would be on the other side of the room, in the reclining chair. She would be down to her bra and panties, not watching us, but reading. Occasionally I would peek over at her. Bunny would read manga. Or sometimes Issac Asimov or Mitch Albom or a book on finance. My intent in looking was not sexual, but an inherent curiosity. See, if I were in her position watching us, I would, well, give anything to join. My body would have to be atomically bonded to that recliner to prevent me from getting some of it.

Yet there she was, hands fixed solely on turning the page, scratching her nose, or adjusting her glasses. Not once did she feel herself or bite her lips. Even the times we would make brief eye contact, she would have the same look she would give me when something interesting happened that day at her work.

How was her vagina not the most tangible itch in the cosmos? Was she afraid? Was she numb? Did she really not understand?

It did not bother me and I did not obsess about it. Bunny was in our family and that was just how it went in the bedroom. We would have liked her to join us and she would when we were all done, dressing herself up in flannel pajamas and cuddling with us. If one of us was ready to go again, she would politely get up and pick up wherever she left off in whichever book she was reading that night.

If she began to understand love and relationships better through us, I am uncertain. That was her pitch to join us back in New Orleans when we first met her. All I do know is she never left us. Those frequent nights spent in bed always turned out the same with her reading and us fucking. She was in on it though. Just not sexually. But she was there, and *involved*. Who knew what was going on in her mind?

22

WHEN YOU HAVE A FAMILY like ours, traveling is so easy. We are not designed to buy a house and stay put somewhere. Not everybody is, society. The farther we traveled together the closer we became. Maybe we could grow closer in staying in one place, but being on the road brought a sort of concentrated bonding. Situations arose bringing out parts of a person that would have otherwise never have been revealed.

For instance, as meek as Hudson was most of the time, when it came to travel he had grown assertive, savvy. When we stopped at a bike shop to get tune-ups, the guy was trying to up-sell us. But Hudson stomped his sales pitch and even haggled a deal for all four bikes. It was fun for him. And any challenges we faced, we would help one another with. Hudson could hold his own in a situation like that, but he could not be trusted alone. He was freaked out over the future so much and was always asking how I thought he should proceed with his life and I would say, "With caution and like a man." Tamra often needed to be consoled from her little breakdowns. Bunny did not require a lot of support, but we were always there if she wanted to open up.

This filling in of each other's blind spots is one way I see our family as a logical evolution or practical alternative to the conventional family.

With a conventional family, you have a kid. Even if you are just doing the bare minimum though, that fucker is your responsibility for eighteen years one way or the other. Then, when you feel you have done right by him, you decide he has got to go, but you still must worry about him all the time. Except he hates you and is unappreciative of your care. So now you are all alone again. A fifth of your life was sucked away for nothing but a legacy of being an asshole.

Conventional families accrued debt and invested in college funds and stayed broke, unfulfilled, and trapped their entire lives. These families sat at a dinner table to plan when they could actually have quality time.

Our family could dress and feel however we wanted.

Both types of families have established rules, that are inevitably broken. But with conventional families, punishment is dolled out to the offender. Our family first understands the reason why and lets the offender absorb the responsibility of her deeds.

Our family, though, does have lies. Menacing truths on par with Santa Claus and the omission of the world's true ugliness.

Punishment might not really solve anything. Children are inherently irrational so there are no other options. That is how my parents thought and look, I am everything they do not want me to be. I am not going to attribute it to the strict punishments, but I will always question, what if? Why did I need to choose these people rather than staying with the ones I was born with? What if punishment only opens a need for reciprocity and just becomes a cycle of pain and torture between both parties. What if there is a better way? If there is, I am not aware of it. But Tamra had to do *something*. Because I forgive her. And it is not fair.

"Don't worry," Bunny tells me as I admit that to her along another road in our hammocks. It is getting warmer outside. "I still have to."

"And so does May," I add.

"She will when we see her. I just know it." It is not so cold out here. Before Hudson wakes up, she whispers to me, "When Hudson finds out, he will forgive us, right?"

"He will have to," I say. "That kid cannot stand on his own."

PART THREE:
HUDSON

23

"IT'S DEAD, HUDSON," TAMRA SAYS to me. Walking over, actually getting up for this, she takes the lighter from me and ignites it. I inhale another hit of the stupid blunt.

"Here," Gary says, lending her a hand by blocking the wind. Together they shield the long blunt containing THC amongst other things, and I take another deep hit. I let it out soon after.

Bunny is laying down on a picnic bench in the grass, a stretch of land presumably gutted out for some human desire to sit. I wish I was her out there, timid yet firm. Sought by all, obtained by none. I feel like the opposite of her. She is beauty and brains. She has reverence for life, the objective valuing of all facts notwithstanding. She didn't even hate me for what I did.

Most of all, she didn't abandon me. I abandoned her though. And I never deserve forgiveness.

So I smoke with Tamra and Gary, what difference did it make since I'd get side-stream smoke from them anyway. My lungs didn't give a shit why there's smoke in them, only that it's there. So I embraced what I didn't want.

I do that a lot.

Most of my life has been large chunks of uneventful monotony. I grew up in Plymouth, Indiana which might be one of the only things duller than I am. My parents brought me up and I had a lot of fun as a kid. Birthday parties, reading *Arthur,* going to Disneyland. The snow was always my favorite. Just being out in it was enough for me. When I got older my friends started going skiing, and I got left behind after the first few times because I wasn't interested. I was happier sitting inside after playing in the snow, sipping hot cocoa. I vegetated, watched *Dexter's Laboratory* or played *Gex* on the PlayStation. After we moved to Lafayette, I had trouble making friends and so made a point of being silent. I stayed focused in school, doing my work and keeping to myself. I think other kids like me were bullied a lot, but I was invisible and I believe that was worse. It was life, and I was only passing through. My grades were good, but I wanted to take a year off after I graduated. The cold had started getting to me. I wondered why anyone would voluntarily choose to live in such a miserable climate as Indiana.

I started working at a movie theater my junior year and was able to start squirreling away money. I had no ties, bonds, or obligations to anyone in Indiana besides my family, but I realized it was from them that I received the mentality to shut up and do all my work. My dad was a supervisor at an aluminum processing factory and my mother was a manager at a steakhouse. They still are.

Girls just kept leaving me. I guess I was kind of busy working, dreaming of where I needed to go besides Indiana. I think my parents were expecting me to go to college right away like everyone else, but they didn't mind it much when I told them I was taking some time off, since I had to no idea what to do with myself. There was this girl that solidified my decision. Her name was Shannon, and she screwed me up good. I don't want to get into it but let's just say she was cheating on me for the entire time we were together and I had no idea.

Something in my subconscious gravitated towards a party city to spend my year in. L.A., Miami, New Orleans. I didn't drink back then, but I wanted to shake things up. To experience an oblivion, a more potent feeling than my experience with Shannon. I chose New Orleans.

I moved into a bad neighborhood and once I was settled I was certain I was going to be shot and taken for my last four dollars. Instead, I got mugged a few months after, when I had more than four dollars.

I needed work. I'd do anything— clean toilets, wash dogs, drive a bus— I just needed something. A series of Craigslist ads led me to Barter's.

The first time you see the French Quarter nightlife, it's glamorous, accelerating, the biggest party you've ever seen. A few times down Bourbon though, and you get desensitized. It gets harder to enjoy yourself in the French Quarter if you're working there. All the places had security, a team of guys waiting for something to go down but until then they were just watching the clock, trying to get people into their clubs or girls into their pants. Most of them were big, bad-ass guys, but that's the job I wanted. One time, this giant black guy named Benjamin and I were talking about girls, about how I didn't like to pick them up just for one-night stands and about standards. He scoffed, saying, "It all feels the same, baby."

"Huh?"

"Pussy. All pussy feels the same. Ugly girls, pretty girls. It don't matter."

I was awe-struck, but remained in favor of monogamy, if for no other reason than I was stubborn. Or maybe I felt the sex and connection would always be superior. I even felt that way during the best sex of my life with Tamra and May.

The general manager at the time, Ana, became such a force in my life. An inspiration being who appreciated me, but her job left her too busy for us to ever talk. In retrospect, I can't blame her. Ana was so precocious, ready for anything. Once I understood her, I recognized what an amazing leader she was. I wondered what a Christian woman from Utah was doing running a bar on Bourbon Street. It didn't seem to add up. Whatever motivation she had I knew was wise and I loved trying to get it out of her. There was a great synergy with everyone she worked with.

It all came down to working as much as possible to cover my expenses. I'd chipped away at my savings getting down there. Looking back most of the people there were saturated in the party atmosphere, and I almost became a victim of that myself.

My high comes down and we mount our bikes to take on the incline we'd been postponing. Gary and I race while Bunny and Tamra walk their bikes. He's hissing at me like an angry goose, but it's amusing as we're neck in neck until I push just a little harder, advancing as the road dips back down again. I stop pedaling and let my legs hang. The view consists of some slice of the Appalachian Mountains. We're around the Shenandoah Valley, an off-shot of the Great Appalachian Valley, a path traversed for millions of reasons since prehistory. Before May, before shoes, before language. Gary, Bunny, Tamra, and I are just the latest adventurers to travel this way.

I was not impressed by today's temperature, but the mist we saw hang in the sky far above the trees and the mountains made up for that. It augmented the intoxicating air I filled my lungs with, clearing out the weed. I'm going to smoke again, but I don't like it. The cloudy day left us a cue to don our trash bags ponchos.

I've never been out this way, but I should have been sooner. There's so much more color, a vivacious backdrop that make Indiana's yellow patches of bumpy fields look sickly in my mind.

While I'm sure the others were impressed with what they saw, they were holding out for another kind of beauty. Contrary to all known sagely advice, this trip is not about the journey, it is about the destination. Without the ability to teleport or time travel, the rest of it is just an obstacle. And with Maryland only a couple of days away, we had better realize that all we can really see is May.

24

SOMETHING ABOUT THE WAY TAMRA is sucking down that Diet Mountain Dew makes me realize how much weight she's lost. We've had sex a few times since reuniting (Gary and I double-teamed her the other night), but this is the first time I've actually noticed a difference in her figure, and I like it.

Then there's Bunny. Oh, Bunny is so beautiful even though she has no chest. That doesn't matter. May is tall, scrawny, and has bigger boobs than Bunny. I've never seen Bunny's boobs. I'm sure Bunny has though… I think.

We filled the air up in Tamra's rear tire but it does no good, just as we feared. It took us an hour of walking our bikes to find a gas station.

We ask around for a Walmart or a bike shop for a new tube.

"The best idea would be to split up," Bunny says. "Tamra and someone go the seven miles to the bike shop before it closes, and two of us stand-by."

That makes me uncomfortable. "What if something happens?" I ask Bunny.

"She's absolutely right, Hudson. None of us want to walk seven miles."

"So who gets the break and who gets to ride?" Gary says.

No one jumps at the opportunity.

"Wait, let's camp around here and get the new tire first thing in the morning," I say. "Then the ones that go can head back to wherever we're camped?"

"Why don't we try hitching to the place?" Tamra suggests, getting anxious.

"Then we'd have to hitch back, Tamra," Bunny says.

"We're just better off in the long run doing this."

"This is getting ridiculous," says Gary. It just keeps going on and on. The frustration of a flat bike, the detours, the egos. As much as I love being in nature, my body is ravaged.

We decide that Tamra and I will go to the bike shop immediately.

Gary is grinning at Bunny. "Time off for us, Bunny."

"That's nothing to be happy about, Gary," Bunny says back to him, perturbed.

Tamra takes Gary's red mountain bike and leaves her purple one with him. We designate the gas station as the rendezvous point. It really sucks not having phones.

While we are riding, I go as fast as I can since the whole splitting-up thing is uncomfortable to me, but Tamra insists I slow down.

She and I never got along well, and now our relationship is mostly sexual. It makes me feel shitty, but I really enjoy her in bed. Since she knows me so well, she also doesn't like me to use a condom. She says there's no way I'd have an STD. As for pregnancy, she has no problem getting another abortion. I've been using one lately, though, considering she cheated on us in Denver.

Tamra is ruthless in terms of a hypothetical pregnancy. She sees anything developing in her womb not as a child, but as a parasite. And since she doesn't want children, she has no problem ruining her womb. She had one abortion, before our relationship. There had been no hesitation and she wouldn't hesitate to get one again. She didn't care about the poor thing, not even for a second. I asked her once, "What if your mother had thought the same of you?

She said, "Then I wouldn't exist to care I never existed."

From then on I tried my best not to get her pregnant. It was like a surgical procedure exiting her vagina and making sure no semen had escaped me. I feel like if I did get a girl pregnant, the life deserved some consideration. That's the way May saw it. But not Tamra. On top of all that, she's against birth control for how terrible it is to the body.

She was obsessed with the end of the world. Though she didn't condescend to believe she'd be one of the survivors of the first wave of whatever end might come our way, she wasn't going to be subjected to parasites.

As faraway as I am from Tamra on most topics, we were close. We debate more than anyone else in our family. But fuck it, I figure it's how we express our love to each other.

25

BACK IN NEW ORLEANS, EVERYONE I tried to get to know blew me off. Barter's was just the wrong place to find friends, but that's the only place I'd go because I hated going out alone, so I fucked myself over.

Good news was that since I was such a good employee, the bar manager Cal promoted me to doing bottle services instead of security. It was more work, but it paid more too.

I was excited, but on my first night he told me to set one up and I didn't have any idea what I was doing and he showed me his temper. But I got the hang of things.

One night, he dared me to walk up to a group of hot girls on the street and try to get them onto the patio for a free bottle service. We set up these outdoor couches with dirty cushions.

Part of that dare stemmed from my inability to approach women. On one end of things I had to man up and approach not just one girl, but a whole group. And they *had* to be hot. This was my job. I had to rely on my substance, my words. There was no attracting them with my muscles or my good looks, because I had none. After ten minutes of walking up and down the street mostly avoiding the hot girls I saw, I finally got a group to bring back.

An exhilarating power came over me when these bachelorette parties agreed to my terms. In that moment I proved myself wrong. I *can* talk to girls. I became the go-to guy to get beautiful women from the street to hang out on our patio. It became the fastest and easiest way to fill up the club.

The girls adored me. I served them, and tips started to come out of nowhere. I never asked anything of them, they just loved me and since I hooked them up with liquor, they gave back. The tips, combined with my wages, were more than double anything I made at any other job. But all that love was not what I wanted. Instead it hurt being loved and revered in that way, because I wanted a relationship, a girl in my life. It was a glossy Bourbon Street fake-out. The girls loved me for what I could provide them, not for who I was. Still the coolest job I ever had. I learned to adapt. If I couldn't find love, I'd worry about money. I flirted with them only as a means to ensure a tip. I didn't want to fuck them for one night and never see them again. It was empty, meaningless. I started getting into drinking then. The job was making me unhappy but the pay was so good I stuck it out. As the months went by I spent most of my time at Barter's, and I remained alone. I couldn't figure it out. Ana and Cal called me in a lot and I'd help them out because I knew how stressed out they were. There was a high turnover rate at a club like Barter's. It was the nature of Bourbon Street.

Then there was this girl across the street at the fried chicken place. I would be outside of the gate at Barter's looking at her and she'd be looking back at me. We did this for a few weeks. At least I thought that's what it was. It was such a relief, at least until I approached her one day and realized what she'd been looking at all those times wasn't me, but the television on the wall which faced Barter's.

My time there is mostly fond memories. Seeing the vapor descending from the balconies of Bourbon Street, wondering how a bra got on the roof at Barter's, sleeping in my hammock there for the entire week of Mardi Gras. But Mardi Gras is when things went bad.

26

THIS ALONE TIME WITH TAMRA gives me a chance to tell her all about my life lately. We have the tube, so we're on our way back. Each conversation results in a clash in our personalities. I don't like it, but it needs to happen. I need to defend what I believe, she taught me that. How else can I know for sure that what I want is really what I want? True beliefs formed true desires, after all.

"When I'm in a relationship," I tell her, "masturbation isn't an issue. When I'm single, it hurts. I feel guilty if I'm watching porn. It makes me feel like a loser."

"What if I watched porn with you?"

"I don't like the exploitation of women that goes on. It's not right."

"It's their choice, not yours. All you have to do is enjoy it, Hudson."

"It's different for you. You're a girl, see? If you wanted sex that bad or whatever you could get it."

"Or whatever? Yeah, I can get laid but it's harder for women to get what they really want than it is for men. So yeah, I'll watch porn if I want."

"Watching porn stifles my confidence. Month, years can go by when I am alone and stuck and I don't get any."

"You have to have a release though," she says. "It doesn't matter how. You can't just not masturbate. I think that's repressive and unhealthy."

"So it feels good then I just feel bad afterward. The things I would get off to are like amateurs making videos to their boyfriends who were assholes and uploaded them online. I pretend that I'm the boyfriend and we're in love."

"It's the dumb bitch's fault. Don't be so sensitive. Maybe

if you tried just hooking-up with people once and a while it wouldn't be so rough. Or at least find porn that you know involves all consenting individuals."

"No, Tamra. Come on. We have each other now, we're in love. Each other is all we have."

"You have yourself too, but I know how much you want to be rid of that."

"Okay, if you only had yourself how could you settle for less if you know how great it is to have been in love?"

"Because I get horny."

"You just can't control yourself. That's why you cheated on us in Denver!" She's ahead of me on the road and doesn't look back. I guess she can't believe I went there. I go even further. "That's why May left, I'll bet."

"Fuck you! You're the one who bitched and bitched all the time. You should have left. We would have been fine. I never wanted to close the relationship. Neither did May or Gary. It's funny though because none of us even fucked with anyone else when it was open."

"Well, we all voted, so if you didn't like it, you're the one who should have left."

"May never would have stayed without me," Tamra says.

"You were there when she left, weren't you? You cheated and that's why she left."

"She never found out, you fucking moron! You can blame everything else on me, but not that, Hudson."

"Great, I look forward to telling her then."

With that settled, I focus on my attention on the road. So does Tamra. We keep biking without a break into the night. Some cars beep at us, but we go faster. As we're about to converge on Gary and Bunny, Tamra says to me, "It was no one's fault that May left."

27

AS GARY AND TAMRA ARE having sex in the lake nearby, I admit to Bunny that I don't like men. It was a con the entire time.

"Everyone figured as much, Hudson," she says. I've lied to them this entire time. It's worse than Tamra, because at least you know she's going to screw you over. Bunny and I are at the top of some stone tower and I had to tell the truth, especially since we're this close to May. "What I want to know is, what are you going to do?"

Yes, it's on me. She'll have no part in it. "When May, Tamra, and Gary messaged me online, I didn't reply for a week because what they said to me upset me so much."

"And what did they say?"

"They wanted me to be happy. That they were happy and I could be happy too. My sexuality wasn't even listed on that site but what they saw from me convinced them that I was they needed. And May was so beautiful... Tamra too. The thought of being with one of those girls... well, you know. I could have them both if I just faked it a little with Gary... so I did."

"Yeah, you went all out then. I've seen you go down on him."

"Well, two girls I'd never get otherwise. What can I say? I sucked it up. I went with them, some polyamorous relationship I didn't believe in and I never even really felt good about it. Then I tried to isolate May. But I failed, like everything else."

"Then I came along."

"Yeah," I say. "It was a lot worse before you came along." Bunny wants more details about what happened with May before I left, but Gary and Tamra return so we stop talking. I guess for now she'll keep things quiet. Or maybe she won't and I'll be exiled. Abandoned again. Why did I tell Bunny any of that?

28

ONE OF THE ONLY FRIENDS I made in New Orleans was this chubby security guard named Johnny. Johnny invited me to go to Pensacola with him one night right after we got out of work. I was so excited to get out of the city for the first time in months, so I went for it. We got in his car, his girlfriend driving. She was pregnant and smoking some weed. Johnny put on Insane Clown Posse after he passed me the joint I pretended to smoke. I shouldn't have taken up this guy's offer.

Johnny spent most of the drive to Florida talking about how much he missed smoking meth. His girlfriend added how aggravating it was that pseudoephedrine was so regulated nowadays.

These people were despicable, not to judge. And they were bringing a child into the world? They were together to be shitty people? No, no. It wasn't right. That child was doomed.

The whole reason we were going to Pensacola was that the last time the two of them were there they found some hotel room key and concocted a plan to use it to sneak into the continental breakfast. Not the worst crime in the world, and I think about trying it now with the others, since we're generally hungry. But with Johnny we had Hawaiian t-shirts. We blended in. There wasn't really anyone to stop us, no one checked our bogus room key card and we spent an hour eating cereal and using their waffle machine.

I brought my hammock so we set up on the beach outside of the hotel after we were done stealing food. All the lawn chairs on the beach were guarded by some guy from the hotel who charged sitting on them by the half-hour. With so many empty lawn chairs, you'd think Johnny would try to haggle with the guy, but instead we just headed back to New Orleans. Johnny and I were exhausted from work and it was clear I wasn't their kind of people.

There was this gas station we stopped on along a country road. After his tank was filled, Johnny went into the store and walked out with a twenty-four pack of Heineken. The guy peeled out, turned to me, and said, "Guy wasn't paying attention and he pissed me off, so do want some free beer?"

He put on this country music, which I actually liked because it calmed me down. Something about powdered milk biscuits.

You hear about these kind of people, or see them in movies, but for Johnny to actually run off with a case of beer was beyond belief. My anxiety kicked in, like what if the cops found us and it turned into some high-speed chase? Butt-fuck it. I took a beer. The case was for display so it was warm. I only had one.

After that, I decided I'd be better off not hanging out with Johnny anymore.

29

SETTLING IN FOR A FEW days at the tower sets me under constant paranoia that Bunny will spill the truth to Tamra and Gary. That my frequent trips to the creek alone will end with me returning to find them gone, moved on to see May without me. In a way I wish for it. It's no more than I deserve. If Bunny doesn't tell Gary, I will. After May.

I feel dizzy tonight. My stomach tries to come up but it's only dry heaves. I wonder if Tamra drugged my hot dog with one of her moon rocks earlier. It would add up, since she volunteered to cook.

All three of them could be conspiring against me, and they should. I was conspiring against them the entire time we were actually together—supposedly happy to be a part of the family, all the while coveting May. I felt so sure May and I could have a normal, happy life together. Kids, pets, refrigerator magnets. None of this polyamorous nonsense.

Sink baths and rolling around in creeks aren't doing it for me anymore. Being dirty is the worst part of traveling. I wish I was some frontiersmen, ages before indoor plumbing, unfettered by my stench and grime. Their sweat was honorable, they didn't want to part with it. Some of them figured it kept away the really bad bacteria.

I go back to the others and they're still here.

Bunny looks over to me. It's a light-hearted moment and I know that she hasn't spilled the beans. Her hair is damp. "I miss your short hair."

"She looked like a boy," Tamra says.

"I miss it too, Hudson," says Bunny with an endearing grin. "Remember when May dressed up like me for Halloween?"

"Oh totally," I say. May loves wearing suits. "Identical hairstyle, dressed in your clothes." When I undressed May that night, I imagined it was Bunny. But those forbidden thoughts, they are the ones I can't ever tell.

30

WHAT SET ANA OFF MORE than anything else was stealing. I was glad when Johnny was gone. All I ever saw him steal was crackers for our gumbo, but I wouldn't be surprised if that's what Ana fired him for. In the midst of Mardi Gras she and Cal were addressing the staff at the end of the night, talking about how thieves were coming into the club when it was busy, orchestrating plans to steal people's phones. Ana was livid that it was happening again.

"What if we turned the lights up in the club?" I suggested. "It's pretty dark in here and it would help us see if someone was going into purses."

"Out of the question," Cal said.

"Why?"

"Because all bars thrive off dim lighting. It's call the ugly lights," Ana explained. "If the patrons can't see how ugly the people they're taking home are, they'll buy them more drinks."

"That's right," said Cal. "No one would hook up with each other if they could see what they looked like in good lighting."

It seemed too silly to be the truth, but there it was. Just like the go-go dancers and the girls on the patio, Barter's has coldly calculated the best way to coerce its patrons into spending more money.

Mardi Gras continued and the same thieves seemed to be coming back each night. The security guards didn't care, since some of them were high. The job was eating Ana alive. She had no time to herself and new obstacles were always coming up. Most of the time it looked like she was five minutes from a nervous breakdown. Nothing could keep her in good spirits.

Three days into Mardi Gras Cal, Ana, and I were all sleeping at Barter's. Something happened while I was sleeping, because when I woke up, Ana was gone. She seemed off earlier that morning, but I never imagined she'd just walk out. Having slept right through her defection, I never saw her again. Ana seemed like family to me, but the entire time she'd been an overwhelmed boss running a business, unable to do anything with herself besides get ready for the rest of that day.

Her abandonment of the job foreshadowed my own. It was Ana who would pep me up when I was so lovesick and annoyed from dealing with all the bachelorette parties. The end of Mardi Gras was such a hollow victory as a parade of police and street sweepers came down Bourbon Street, closing the street up. That week had brought us all to the point of delirium, and we all missed Ana so much. Cal assumed her role at Barter's. He told me there had been no goodbye. She just slipped out and wouldn't return. I thought that was good. If things had been that bad for her, it was for the best that she stayed away.

I ended up leaving New Orleans for Winston-Salem, North Carolina, devastated.

Bars elude me. Stuff like the ugly lights and marking up the drinks. Still people pay. Then you're supposed to buy girls drinks and hope they'll talk to you. It's stupid to go to a bar. Not if you work at a bar though, it's definitely worth it, even if I still have emotional backlash from those bachelorette parties. A lot of those brides didn't deserve to get married. I saw them making out with guys from the club or behaving as if they were single. Why do some people get to have to partners when I don't? Why do some people get to find the one they want to marry and then cheat and I don't get anyone? I guess that's why I went for May, Tamra, and Gary. Butt-fuck it. It's not like I can get what I want. Not like Johnny. All these awful people in love and me, all alone. I would never cheat. Tamra can probably cheat all she wants and get away with it. My belief is in true love through monogamy. I don't know if it's indoctrination or I'm just hurt or biased or jealous, but May should have been mine. I should have been all she needed.

31

AFTER WE CROSS THE SUSQUEHANNA River, entering Pennsylvania, Tamra and Gary light up a new joint while riding, while we're right out in public where everyone can see. I ride over to them and say, "What the fuck?"

"What?" Gary asks nonchalantly, lighting the thing up. "Oh, you want some?"

"No!" It's clear that Bunny has not divulged my secrets, including that I hate smoking weed and it bothers the shit out of me that they do it non-stop. Yet most of the time I'd share it with them when they offered it. Bunny isn't susceptible to that, though. She doesn't like to smoke so she never did. And they respect that. It's different for me though. I don't think I could have the same respect she has because she's more than I am.

"Why not?" Tamra asks me. "Just relax, Hudson."

"What if police see you?" I point out.

"Quit worrying about it," says Gary.

"Oh? And if not? You're going to let Bunny suffer because you guys needed to get high? They'll take her in too you know. Biking on this road stoned. Idiots."

"What's your problem, man?" Tamra questions me. "You're usually down and chill. I don't think even Bunny cares, do you Bunny?"

"I'm completely indifferent," Bunny says behind us.

"Just have a little, huh buddy?" Gary asks, coordinating to pass the joint to me with one hand and continuing to ride with the other. "What if that?"

"No! If you keep offering me, I'm going to say keep saying no!" I don't even know how they still have weed, weeks out from New Orleans.

"Fine, whatever."

"Look, this is slowing us down."

"Hudson, it doesn't make that much of a difference," Bunny says. "We'll be in Doylestown tomorrow and get the car either way." She smiles at me. I have no idea what that means. "That's all we want. Let them enjoy their drugs and stuff."

I let it go.

They'll tell me how I need to relax and not worry so much, and how weed is just the thing for me. It's legal in Colorado, and I almost think that's why Tamra and Gary pushed Denver so fucking much after we were fed up with New Orleans. They wanted to move our family just because of the legalization. Dumb marijuana culture's the real apocalypse Tamra's worried about, and she was a victim of it.

Regardless, Denver, was the golden age of our family (despite it being an endpoint). I became numb to the polyamorous stuff, pleasuring Gary enough so he wouldn't be suspicious, even initiating private hook-ups with him. Everyone just kind of kept doing their thing; it wasn't like there was a slow decline to a break-up. Come to think of it, if May's mother hadn't been dying I bet things would still be dandy. Denver wasn't so bad at all. It was better than any other time of my life. Our place wasn't even smoky, out of respect for Bunny. She did have to speak up about it though, those dicks.

We'd go out a lot, see the local music uptown or stay pent up in our apartment. The sex was phenomenal. I assume that's why we're all headed toward May, as I argue Gary and Tamra.

They finally tell me the truth.

"We found out in New Orleans, Hudson," Gary says. "May is dead."

32

I HATCHED THIS CRAPPY PLAN once to spend the night alone with May and pitch her our life together. It was a Wednesday in Denver, and I had to take off work and make sure she had no plans. We had sex, just the two of us. It wasn't often it was just the two of us. We started off in the shower, then moved to the bed. After I came, I asked what was so great about this life, the five of us? What the initial germ was of this idea?

"I believe it was a reaction to seeing to many people with unchangeable beliefs," May told me. "Close-mindedness inhibits growth." Her wavy hair crawled across the pillow with her as she shifted to the side. Some of it got on me. I smelled lemons. "People just need to try everything they can and never dismiss possibilities. That's why I'm so proud of you, Hudson." She gives me a kiss.

"Of me? Why?"

"You gave this a try. We knew you'd never been in a relationship like this, but look how it turned out. You're not alone anymore. There's so much love coming to you, to make up for the lack you've always struggled with. And Bunny is here and everything is as it should be."

"But what about later? A few years from now? Are we just going to stay together now?"

"If you want to try, so do I," she said. "Right now I'm the happiest I've ever been in my life. I'm assuming that comes off of me. The day we met Bunny, well you know."

"Yeah. But what if it wasn't the five of us."

"What do you mean?"

"May, I love you the most."

I was staring at her back but she wouldn't turn to face

me. "Ex-excuse me?"

"I want a monogamous relationship with you. Let's start from scratch. Tell me what it would take to make that even a faint possibility."

"Hudson... no. I believe in our family and you should too. We can't regress into roles as breeders and consumers, conforming to norms because our parents expect it of us. We have to seek out what is best for us. This is where I belong. Not just with you, but with Gary, Tamra, and Bunny too."

"But aren't you just deliberately challenging every convention of society? Mindlessly question authority at every turn? I bet all the guys you were with were just assholes. I'm not, you know? I could be what you need and you don't even think about it."

"Slow down, Hudson. Look at the apartment we have now. None of us has great income, but we split the rent five ways. It's nice to have extra cash. We don't have to worry about finding friends as much, so wherever we go it happens gradually, without stressing us out. Then we have the options to sleep with Tamra or Gary or just cuddle with Bunny. And we're all in love, Hudson. I love us."

"I love us, too. But I don't know if this is right for me anymore."

"Of course it isn't. Neither is me breaking up our family just for you. Like dude, we changed everything for you." She was getting angry out of nowhere, getting out of bed and getting dressed. I focused on the disappearing parts of her body, her vagina being enveloped by purple panties, her Nine Inch Nails shirt draping over her head, a shield against me seeing her breasts. "Now you're trying to break it after that? We closed this relationship so your narrow mind could handle it. None of us wanted that, but we fucking did it for you. You want to break this family, the only thing that's going to happen is you're going to be asked to leave. In fact, I would get ready for that." May grabbed her bottle of Jack Daniels and took a very long swig.

"May, for God's sake, you're the one who needs to slow down," I said, getting up.

"My mother is dying! And you want me all to yourself? I need everybody right now. My family. Bunny, Gary, Tamra. Well, maybe not you, if this is you."

"I can stay. I belong here. I want to be here."

I tried to kiss her, but her lips were stiff, dry, and motionless to mine. "It doesn't matter how good of a liar you are if I already know the truth."

"May, please," I said. And she was so shaken up at the time about her mother that she just let it be.

Then like Ana a few days before Mardi Gras, May left us without a word. Different people, the same exact feeling of abandonment. We all knew about her mother and felt she shouldn't go. But it's funny, how whenever we make a decision together, there's always a quiet unrest that explodes into something like this. I wholeheartedly believe May left because of me.

When I was about to go to Maine after her, she told me, "Don't you dare, Hudson. I don't want to see you."

She didn't know I wasn't with them anymore because I was already on my way to her from Indiana, staying with my parents for a few days before I took a bus all the way to Maine. She disconnected from everyone after that. All that time passed us by. And I stayed at my parent's waiting for her acceptance like a fool, assuming she had come clean to Tamra, Gary, and Bunny about everything. Until I found out that Tamra and Gary were coming to meet me, completely unaware of what had happened. But then again, so was I.

33

BY THE TIME WE REACH Doylestown it's too late to get our rental car, so we camp out by a bridge near the rental car place. We haggle with the YMCA to let us use their shower.

Things have been tense since they confessed May's death to me. All the ugliness was out there. We even missed her funeral. Back in New Orleans they'd been corresponding with May's family, but May's family were jerks.

In the shower, Gary starts telling me how great Bunny and I are for each other. "Too bad she's asexual, huh asswipe?" Yep, it's all out there now.

"Huh?"

"I should want to kill you. You tried to… on top of her and everything."

"Dude, no. It wasn't like that. I stopped. I misread that situation." It was so long ago, funny how it comes out now, with everything else. I hadn't even wanted to admit what had happened between Bunny and I that time to myself.

"You are not even a bit gay. I knew it."

"Then why'd you keep me around? I must be a little gay, considering everything we've done together."

"I do not know what May wanted from you. She always stuck up for you. If we had just picked someone other than you, we would not be here now. I bet May, Tamra, and I would still be in Denver."

"But you still fell for me," I argue. This is a strange argument to have, because we're both naked, whispering to one and other in the YMCA men's locker room.

"Our whole family was a lie," Gary concludes. He's quiet after that, and I wonder if he could possibly be wrong.

After the YMCA, we pawn our bikes.

"Are we seriously doing this?" Tamra asks us a block away from the rental car place. "After everything?"

"We have no money moving forward," Bunny says.

"We are just going to have to do whatever it takes to get to Maine," Gary says. "Except lie. So there is no need to keep the formalities going. Hudson, you can leave now if you want." His eyes squinted at me.

"Hang on now—" I try to interject, but he's not interested in what I have to say. I was going to say I doubt they could get the rental car without my share of money.

"Maybe you do not deserve to see May. And she would not want to see you. She told us how you asked her for it just to be the two of you too."

I feel far away from the others. Tamra comes to my defense for a moment then tells me I'm a little shit and I need to speak for myself. She shoves me. I pull it together.

"Gary, you think this family is better than any other family," I say, not believing I can get the words together through my proliferating anxiety. "But maybe we're just no different. We all do bad things to each other and are expected to forgive. I've deceived you all more or less from the start, but I think May wanted me in and she knew how it was going and there was something about it she didn't care about. I like to think she accepted me and still wanted to make sure I didn't feel alone even in the middle of all my conflicting ideologies (like, just because I felt different she thought it didn't mean I had to be alone). But whatever. The things we've done and the times we've spent together, it doesn't change the fact that we're family. I am not going anywhere, because I need to say goodbye to May. Understand that we still have one last thing to take care of. *Together.* And I still love us. And I forgive myself and whatever it is you've all done to each other and me."

"I feel the same," says Bunny. "This is how we must find and face May. As healed and reconciled beings in harmony."

"I will not just forgive him on the spot!" Gary says, tears

coming out as he breaks downs and crashes into Tamra, who lifts him up as his knees bend.

Dusting his dirty jacket off, Tamra says, "He doesn't have to be. But fuck it. I'm the one who needs to be forgiven for cheating. Something inside me knew May was already gone. I didn't know why she— she was the centerpiece of this. We all know it. Look what happened right after she left. Hudson was the one who orchestrated us getting back together, not me. I've been taking credit for it and hating Hudson for staying away from us those three months and—"

"Tamra, it's okay," I say.

"No!"

"I don't know if we're starting over, but we shouldn't stand on the side of the road like this," says Bunny. "We can do all this in the car, getting closer to May."

"I know, I know," says Gary. He looks up at me. "You are your own person, Hudson."

"No."

"Yes. Think about that. You are not supplementary for me or a boy toy for a relationship. You are you. On your own. An individual."

Bunny and Tamra help Gary as I lead the way. An hour later we drive off in a Camry, four hundred seventy-nine miles to go.

PART FOUR:
BUNNY

34

I HEARD FOR THE FRONT seat, having filled up the tank gas without any incident. But then Hudson and Tamra stop me.

"It's okay, Bunny. I'll keep driving," says Tamra.

"It's my turn," I say.

"We know," says Hudson. "It's just, you haven't slept."

"Oh. So what?"

"How long's it been, two days?" Tamra asks.

"Lay down in the back with Gary," Hudson suggests, reaching his arm out to get the door open.

"No," I say. "I'm driving now."

"Bunny," Tamra says.

"It's my turn." I make it to the driver's seat and start the car. They're behind me yelling. "What is it, loves?"

"Still pumping gas back here, turn the engine off!" I hear Hudson say. Ooops. I guess I didn't finish the tank without any incident after all.

Tamra motions for me to roll down the window. I hold the button down for about a second and Tamra slips some caffeine pills to me. I take three at once and look at a man who is walking his Doberman. The dog doesn't realize it, but I love him or her.

"We're going to help you along the way," says Hudson, jumping into the passenger seat through the open window. "I'll be in the front, your navigator."

"Hudson, that's all right. I know, we're just going to curve around New York City. If I need any help, I'll let you know. Cool?"

He leans his seat as far back as he can without disturbing Gary's space. "Yeah, that's fine. See, I'm not one of those overbearing navigators. Only if you need me, Bunny."

Gary is sleeping and Tamra approaches him so she can obtain some cuddles. He will probably feel better after his nap, since he was freaking out earlier. When his turn to drive comes up, Tamra goes next. We established that we'd switch drivers every time we stopped for gas.

It'd be nice if we had a Doberman. I did so much fighting for animal rights when we were in Denver, at least until I realized it didn't make enough of a difference. At the same time, I think I was distracted from doing the things I wanted. Relationships seem to hinder my ability to make independent decisions, and I don't like that. But May's ideas were sound to me. So she would check up on me every now and then, knowing I was really there as a pseudo-partner, learning and trying to understand things.

"So what have you gathered lately?" May asked me one night on an elevator at the mall she used to visit to get her nails done.

"I think this is the only relationship I'll ever be a part of," I told her.

"That's an intense thing to say."

"Not as bad as what you said the a few weeks ago during dinner."

"Which was?" May asked.

"This is closest to most perfect day of my life."

"Oh yeah."

"There are obviously many advantages to customizing a relationship to suit everyone's needs, but I just really don't think I'll find a guy or girl out there who is fine that I don't want to have a sexual relationship. You all accept that more or less, but it's easier since there's four of you and you can divert all your sexual energies onto each other." We got off the elevator and walked to the exit.

"Oh Bunny, I bet there are tons of people like you."

"Tons? Like one percent of the human population."

"Either way. It's totally okay for you to look. I know Hudson might object since he got us to close the relationship, but you know you're a special case. And he's gotten his way enough as it is. I'd hate to see you leave, but if you ever feel like you've found someone else, no love lost."

"Thank you May. But I just don't see it happening. I don't want to search, it just doesn't bother me enough."

"What about long term though, Bunny?" May asked, rubbing my shoulders as we stopped to look into the fountain. "Are you content with the fate of a spinster?"

"Only after you all tire of me. Where is our family ultimately going?"

"I don't answer questions like that, you know? I don't know. And I don't like to guess or lie," said May.

"But what would you want? You must know that."

"I would want to feel the way I did that day at dinner, every day."

"Hmmm."

May leaned into the fountain and scooped out a handful of coins. The people around us watched her suspiciously, the devious lanky girl stealing their wishes away. Really she was taking them and using them as reminders. "People want things, but they don't know what it takes. They think if they give a nickel, it's a fair exchange. Where's my wish, they wonder. I paid good money to that fountain!"

"But you know how to set them straight," I told her.

"That's right. Each of these is going to be a wish of mine that I make come true."

"May, do you take everyone aside for private time and talk to them?"

"Yes. Yes, I do. You know I originally went into school to become a therapist?"

"Yeah. You mentioned that."

"I guess it's still a part of me. Teaching English to people is cool, though. It reminds me of how people throw coins into the fountain and just trust in the universe. Those people assume I'm teaching them good English, and they believe the things I say even if they aren't true because they perceive me as an authority as a teacher. I would have become a therapist if it weren't for people like Hudson."

"What do you mean?"

"It's always about him. And he's sad and disappointed and he won't try things to make it better. He uses all his available energy to complain about his lot. That job he had on Bourbon Street was like a cheat code for life and all he does is hate on the experience, blubbering over Ana. But all that stuff is how he came to meet us. And there's still parts of him that aren't happy somehow. That I just don't understand. I asked him once, what's the first thing you try to find out about a girl you like? He said, if she's loyal. Are you kidding, I thought to myself. I want to know if I find them interesting or boring. That poor fucker."

"It's really dangerous analyzing people so close to you like that."

"I think it's safer than not knowing."

Oh May, I think to myself while driving the final stretch, the detour through Pennsylvania to circumvent the bustling toll-and-traffic-a-thon that is New York. *Didn't you know about your mom?*

35

"GUYS, SERIOUSLY. THIS IS ACTUALLY getting me just a little piqued," I say. "You aren't going to keep Hudson isolated like a rabid dog. We already decided on this."

I can't believe them. They want alone time in the car tonight and they expect me to stay close because apparently Hudson can't be trusted.

"Bunny, I am just trying to look out for you," Gary says.

"He's not a fucking malcontent, he's a lonely, horny kid. That's that. It was just one time."

Yeah, he tried coming on to me before, but I handled it and he's still sorry and guilty about it.

We were cuddling one day alone back in Denver and he started moving around a lot, coming in for kisses. I explicitly explained to all of them that I drew the affection line at kissing. After anything more than peck on the lips, I get very uncomfortable. He started making-out with me. I just didn't move my lips and tightly pressed them together, not saying anything like May taught me. My hands went to his chest to repel, not pushing him away because I still wanted him to cuddle, but I was being naive.

"Bunny," he whispered to me with a hot sigh. I felt something stiff pressed against me.

I didn't lose my temper. I didn't freak out. I couldn't. You had to try and understand people. It was wrong to take offense or get hurt when someone did something you didn't like. Empathy's so important to me. Turning my head away from his attempts to kiss me I told him, "Don't Hudson."

"Try," he told me. "You're so beautiful, don't you feel?"

"Yes. And I love you. But this is wrong. I told you I don't want this."

"Bunny."

"I can stop you whenever I want, but I want to give you the choice to stop yourself. If I have to, you won't like it."

That seemed to get to him. That stiffness in his pants parted from me and he retreated his advance on my body.

"Good Hudson. It's okay. That's not who I am. Remember. I'm not Tamra or May. I'm different."

"I know. But why? Why?! Jesus, you always tease me sitting in your bra and panties just watching us. Don't I turn you on? Am I ugly?"

"Hudson stop. Don't take it personally. I'm a virgin. There's just something in my psychology that isn't particularly interested or doesn't understand that type of exchange."

"It's so hard. You turn me on so much." He takes my hand in his, tightening hard.

"I'm going to take a walk. When I come back, make sure you're taken care of and we can just forget this every happened. You have to, okay?"

"I hate that!"

"It doesn't matter. Do it. I'll give you a twenty minutes." I stepped out with my paperback copy of *The Stand*. It was cool being able to read it so close to Boulder. I wanted to go there someday.

With most secrets about our relationship out, we've all largely forgiven one and other, but Gary and Tamra still persist in being jerks to Hudson in small moments such as this.

"It's going to be fine," I persist.

"No, we need this," says Gary, leaning up against the car trunk.

"Whatever then, so let it go. Hudson will be fine." Hudson has been, incidentally, here the entire time, struck silent by the blatant disregard of his presence.

"Let's just park at that church we smoked in the back of and they can set up camp there," says Tamra. "We'll be near them but still get our privacy."

"What do you even need privacy for?" Hudson asks, breaking his silence.

"We are not trying to keep any secrets from you, man," Gary says. "We just want some time apart. It has been a long road and we need to chill after everything if we expect to be in good shape to see May."

"Goddammit, I thought we already settled that shit," says Tamra to Gary.

"No, we did. Look, forget it okay, Hudson? We know you would not fuck with Bunny."

"So don't."

"Okay," Hudson says, looking down at his shoes.

Together we find a nice spot beyond the church parking lot. There is a clearing and a series of benches and folded chairs locked up by a chain. We have difficulty finding trees to put the hammocks up, so we keep walking deeper into the woods until we both find good ones.

"Remember the wolves howling?" Hudson asks me when we are done with tying the hammocks.

"Of course. I never want to do this again."

"I think it was just we were so far out from any help if something did happen. I don't feel much better about everywhere else we set up camp, but fuck it."

"Maine's going to be all country like that. It's like a Canadian state."

"That's why I say we go to Augusta or another big city in New Hampshire."

"Yeah, right."

Hudson's nibbling on a banana, dipping it into rest of the big yogurt container we were sharing. "You know, there's something I never got a chance to ask you."

"What's that?"

"Well I was on your Facebook once and I saw in some of your picture you looked like a boy."

I laugh and some air pushes out of my nose. "I used to screw with people and tell them it was my twin brother, but really it was me all along."

"So there would be pictures of you in those dresses that looked like a doll would wear, then there was one of you with a Sharpie beard and suspenders. You'd look really sweaty with a manly face or have a wig on."

"That wasn't a wig. I had my hair cut like a boy's."

"Oh. Wow. What do they call that? Androgynous?"

"I guess. It's just annoying to conform to one gender. Yes, I have to deal with periods but I imagine sometimes what it must be like to have a penis."

"It's horrible. You're plagued with a constant need to reproduce. There's no way you've ever felt that."

Hudson doesn't really get asexuality. I don't bother correcting him. "Right."

There's a bit of daylight left and I want to be done with the conversation so I pull out my book. They know when I pull out a book I'm not to be disturbed. Hudson goes into his hammock, throwing the yogurt container and the banana peel on the ground and I make a note to myself to pick it the yogurt container up for him later. He is not the way to be, but I'm not finished with him yet.

36

MY LIFE HAS BEEN PUNCTUATED by a constant need to be surrounded by cuteness. Puppies in blankets or anime girls like Bulma and Mihoshi. I devoured manga. I always had a pet, whether it was a guinea pig, a hamster, rabbits, a dog, a cat, anything. When one died, my parents wasted no time in taking me to the pet store. It was a constant uninterrupted chain until I was about fourteen and our family cat had to be put down for a tumor. They told me we would get another one, but I asked not to. I was done. It didn't seem right.

I was born in Baton Rogue but I grew out of it very quickly. They weren't many people who had the same interests I did, but that didn't stop the boys from bothering me, coming up to me in the lunch room to find out who I was and why I was sitting alone. It didn't make much difference to me, lunch was twenty minutes and I spent thirteen of those minutes chewing on a sandwich or some pretzels, and the other seven minutes I'd be speed-reading some manga. But I never discouraged or told whoever was sitting near me to go away. I just think they realized I was impenetrable to them and eventually they'd try the bit on someone else. It was sweet of them to not let me sit alone, but what they never seemed to get was I didn't care much either way.

School was easy me, sometimes I was even interested in learning. The size and mystery of the universe has yet to captivate enough people. You know what I think it is? Fear. People who can't get past how scary it is can't take an interest.

Being a girl, I noticed social circles around me forming

and conspiring to do make-up and talk about boys, and it always just went way over my head. Every social calamity such as homecoming and prom were things to be avoided. But I did end up having a circle of friends who were into anime. We had a lot of fun. Once we tried to start a Gay-Straight Alliance, but it turned into this big controversy we were forced to nix. What I remember most about that was while I was livid over our school's denial to have a group like that, my homosexual friends were the ones really discriminated against. I think that gave me more of a reason to fight against things I felt were unjust.

It was also easy to notice in high school the focus shifting into dating, and I just felt very off regarding the whole premise. I felt lonely but at the same time there was no one I met who I felt could change that. I stuck with my studies and got a scholarship at the University of New Orleans, opting to study physics of all things. I was so fascinated, even the tribulation that was AP Physics couldn't stop me. The work was tough, but the knowledge was so enlightening and it hugged me like a person, seeming to make my loneliness all right. After all, we were all ultimately alone. All those boys wanted to know me at the lunchroom and I wanted to know the universe. I'm still hoping the universe isn't as indecisive as I am, because my parents still ask me when I want that next pet.

37

SEXUALITY COMES UP AGAIN IN the car. Straight, gay, whatever. I'm driving again and Gary says, "I do not think there is such a thing as sexuality."

"Oh, not this again," says Hudson.

"What?" Tamra asks.

"Look, if we were all born in Ancient Greece, it would be totally normal to be fucked by old men," Gary says. "Pederasty was just a thing back then. When they went to war, they fucked their fellow soldiers instead of their wives, who were of course back at home. I think a person's sexuality is most commonly based on society. Where you are from, when you are from. I could have been born somewhere and turned out straight. I just so happened to live in Tennessee and something happened where I like men more."

"But what about those people who get sick thinking of the same sex?" Tamra counters.

"I'm actually with Gary on this one," I say, "because I like to think if I was born somewhere else, I'd be like anyone else who wanted to get it on."

"There's nothing wrong with you though, Bunny," says Tamra.

"I'd think not. I'm just on board with Gary here."

"Yeah, nice," says Gary. "Yeah, I'm just saying that society labels us too tightly and it's messed up. Brian Molko once said heterosexuality isn't normal, it's just common."

"Here, here," says Hudson.

"So what, we're all just pansexual?" I ask Gary for clarification. I slow down for tolls into Massachusetts.

"Theoretically, why not? Hudson, think about May for a

second. What if her exact same personality was in a man's body?"

"I don't know, man."

"At the expense of never falling for him?"

"No. It's a hard question is all. But I see your point." The next border was closing in. Three cars left until it's our turn.

"Love does not distinguish for sexuality, so why should we?" Gary goes on. "We are all just born pansexual, and our experiences close possibilities, most of the people are repressed and unwilling to accept other cultures and other things."

"But not me," says Hudson.

"Damn right," says Tamra.

It feels like this discussion is wasted time. I don't value anything more than time. Not love, not money, not happiness. "Whose got change?" I ask the car.

38

TAMRA NEVER THOUGHT, ESPECIALLY GIVEN all those times denying homeless people in New Orleans, that'd she would be the one trying to get some change.

We're hanging out outside of a Bank of America, stuck in Massachusetts. It was all we could do to get the rest of the way to May. The money we saved was almost gone and we considered cutting our loses.

"If only we had blue paint," Hudson says.

"Or we could balance on stuff," Gary says.

"Or we had a Jedi uniform," Tamra says.

I remember all those buskers in New Orleans fondly. There were magicians, musicians, acrobats. I remember this one guy walking around with three parrots always drunk. That bothered me. But I never did get a good look at the French Quarter until we were there a few weeks back.

The University of New Orleans was four miles away from the French Quarter by Lake Ponchartrain, in a part of the city known as Gentilly. I had no idea what to expect, but the scholarship paid for all my expenses so I stayed in the dorms. People were immature, stinky, and wild. I really didn't belong there. The school invited me to join the Honors Club but I just wanted to learn enough physics to be able to come up with my own theories one day. How much money I ended up making after college was sort of inconsequential. That's what bothered me about everyone else. A pure physics major was rare at UNO. I think there were about eight undergrads in the program. Everyone else was going for engineering. Not only that, they all lacked passion. They had ambition for their future, dollar signs in their eyes, just not passion. The present moment or problem was something to learn next, for months and months until they were done and were just competent enough to be hired somewhere where they could make lots of money and pay off all the accumulated debt they'd got from learning how to be qualified and hired for these jobs.

That's how most people looked at it. There was no respect or integrity for the sanctity of education, knowledge. The facts and the information weren't remotely interesting to them, but were only a means to an end. But not for me. I absorbed it too much. I hardly slept back then, staying up doing homework and forming study groups with these people I had no choice but to work with.

This one boy named Curtis began talking to me, bragging about how he had obtained the completed solutions manual to our physics textbook. At first I blew him off because he was just another incarnation of the boys who approached me between classes and while I was eating, but eventually we became friends and tried together to survive the daunting flow of work. Everyone saw him as a bullshitter. He'd often tell everyone he'd get them ice cream but he'd never deliver. When we went to study at the Tulane library late into the nights between beignets, he told me about God and I laughed. God is love, God is science, God is gracious. God would help him graduate, had already provided him with the answers. How wrong-headed. Every song that would come on, he'd say it was my song. He was a sweet boy and had no clue. Just like Hudson. Only difference was that I didn't mind. If he knew now I was in a polyamorous relationship, he'd get it all wrong.

Battling against assignments all the time did not leave much room for social activities. There was a bus that went from Elysian Fields to the French Quarter, but I just never seemed able to get out there and check it out.

The whole experience left a bad taste in my mouth—being surrounded by all these students who had disingenuous motivations. I'll always see an inherent value in truth. In knowledge. It wasn't simply a means to an end. But if you're surrounded by people who feel differently than you, you're kind of muted.

That's why it was such a big deal when I came across these vagabonds on the pier outside of UNO one day. They were with one and other not because they had the same classes, but because they were going through the same life. They loved one and each, going away from what society wanted from them.

I was with Curtis and a few other people trying to find a way to cross the gap in the pier. The concrete pathway was damaged, presumably from some hurricane that had passed through. The pier was a precarious walk with many holes that fell into deep cavities and pieces of concrete that jutted upward. We were all STEM majors, so we treated it like a challenge. Whatever resources we could find nearby were considered. The vagabonds were watching us, scoffing but intrigued. Then they approached and joined us in our lofty goal. It was Hudson, May, Gary, and Tamra. They were waiting for the first so they could move into their new apartment. It was the twenty-sixth.

Curtis, after an hour of finding nothing but a thin stretch of wood and rusted metal rods along a bench, committed to reaching the other side by jumping. We all agreed it was too far to reach in one jump. It was no small fall either. Not so far down that the person couldn't make it back up or to the shore, but a pain nonetheless. So sure of himself, Curtis jumped. It was no good. He came close but never touched the other side. After he fell into the defeat of seawater, we helped to hoist him back up and called our challenge quits.

It was a fun day hanging out with Hudson, Tamra, May, and Gary for the first time. I remember letting them shower in my dorm. They told me they were all together and I didn't understand what they meant at first. My initial guess was they were two couples, that any two of them could have been a couple. They told me the truth and my mind churned with unfamiliar thoughts. I became friends with this family. A kind of connection I've never had was forged.

I couldn't spend much time with them at first, but once my semester was over I saw them every chance I got outside of my internship. They persuaded me to switch from physics to phlebotomy. Something about living in the now. I still want to study physics, that hasn't changed, it was just too much of a beating at the time. Which is a terrible argument because it only gets harder the longer I wait, getting sucked into these sketchy adventures with Hudson, Tamra, and Gary.

When I was away from them in Texas I even considered disconnecting from them, thinking that everything that had happened was a natural conclusion. I would have still felt that way if May hadn't died.

39

WHEN MY PARENTS SAID WE were crazy, they paused, then added empty. Empty and crazy. That really just means they didn't get it, which honestly isn't so bad. I don't know about everyone else, but I'm good with that. Don't take people too seriously; they say one thing but meant a different thing entirely.

Hudson takes over for me at an I-95 rest stop and that Talking Heads song about the days going by comes on the radio. "I love this song," I say. I shut it off before the first chorus and no one turns it back on.

When enough silence elapses, Hudson feels the need to talk. He says, "When I used to make fun of those kids who wore skinny jeans, I was just feeling left out. They weren't leaving me out of shit, still I felt that way. I didn't dislike them. I disliked the idea of people like me making fun of me if I did wear them. I disliked not having what they did. They didn't care what I said, they just wore what they wore."

"More," I say. "We have to finish embracing each other totally."

"Bunny," says Tamra from behind me. "This is as much as we're going to know one and other."

I know what I want to say to Tamra is that she needs to accept the unfavorable parts of Hudson, Gary, and myself. Embrace them all. But I don't know how to say that to her in a way she'll comprehend and implement, so I follow-up with Hudson. "Maybe you'll never get a chance to apologize to them. Or maybe you will and you'll get too scared. But it's okay. They probably figured out the truth."

He's munching on a bagel, bites of guilt as I talk. He likes the sour onion kind the best.

I look out at the land and Gary says, "You need to go to sleep, Bunny. When it is your turn again we will need you to be alert." I bet Tamra is enjoying the scenery of trees and fields more than me because she's high off of her final moon rock. "Bunny," Gary says.

"What?"

"Sleep."

"Maybe."

Earlier, Tamra asked me, "Why are you so benevolent and tender while the rest of us are hateful?"

I think we finally got full truth out of everyone. Tamra cheated on us in Denver, Gary has a holy death wish for Hudson, Hudson's lied all along about things, and me? I'm just here to observe. That's the worst crime out of everyone, in my opinion. I'm an extra, on the periphery, looking in. Detached from many of the emotions the others are experiencing. If I sleep, I can't observe anymore. "This is what is going to happen. This is the world ahead of us."

Hudson is crying in the front seat.

"That's enough, Hudson." I hug him tight.

East. Eventually I want to be able to point to some spot on the road and say, this happened there. No pictures, but this or that happened. Right there.

"Stop thinking you're alone or that you can't have what you really want or that you don't know what that is," I tell Hudson.

"I'm okay," he tells me. "We're okay. It's not me. It's May. May's been all by herself. She's been alone." Since she's been dead, that hasn't been an issue to me.

"We've done everything we could about it," says Tamra. "This was our best." I disagree with her, but don't say so.

"She chose," Gary adds.

"Imagine too," says Hudson. "She could of gone to see you in New Orleans. Or me in Indiana. You know, when we were alive. But no. We're going to see her when she's dead."

I don't want there to be any disagreements ever again.

40

IT WAS THE OPPOSITE OF anything personal, but May hadn't wanted me to join the family.

"We're horny, horrible people who belong with each other," she told me when I asked to be some part of them. It was simple. I had never been in a relationship. I'd never pursued anyone, and utterly ignored anyone who pursued me. "So if that's what you think you want... I don't think it is."

"What I want," I told her, "and I know this is weird, but I want to feel comfortable enough with you all. To be a subsidiary part of your relationship. I want to be let in, so to speak. I don't want to do anything sexual, ever. I would like to be there though. If you would let me watch you all, how you love, why you do. I'm sure that, eventually, it will come to me too. But in the meantime, I only want to be welcome to contribute what I can. Take care of you and your partners, help you all succeed."

"The boys, they..." May trailed off. "I can talk to them about this more." For a relationship that had thought itself closed to new members, the four of them became fascinated with the idea of me. May made it happen. It took a few weeks to receive a yes, but I was in. Time passed and they ended up staying in New Orleans just for me, so I could finish school. They were all interested in Colorado when Hudson found out that belonging was not a place, but the people he was with. And when they left New Orleans for Denver, I went with them. There's always been an interest within for why I happen to be different from everyone else I meet, I guess now I am so much more accepting of it and whatever that comes with, and I have the family to thank for that.

41

WHAT IS AFTER FOR US? Not us. Not some New England city. Just May, then probably nothing.

Maine's border is much like Massachusetts's and New Hampshire's were. The air was different though. This is where May came from. The sight for our failure.

In the back seat with Tamra, I get ready for bed. Hudson had spit his toothpaste out of the window earlier and we couldn't get it off of the car. We are doomed. There are no plans after this. As much as we've all knocked on our parents, they might be our only hope. We'll be beggars for society, comfort, stability. It wasn't that May stood against those things, she just believed in sacrificing those things for more important ones: community, adventure, spontaneity.

The daylight gets on me and I can't get it off. It pierces through my shut eyes, assuring me that no matter how tired I am now it will fight me. A force stronger than me. Same story with the car seat. I shift and Tamra tries to get in close, but I say, "No."

She goes, "Why?"

"I can't sleep with you like that."

"Are you really going to sleep this time?" Gary asks me. My eyes are closed so I hear his voice and where it's coming from, but that's it.

"I'm sure I need to try," I say. This is time I didn't want. But it was the most important time I could think of. The last part of us. And I was going through it warped on caffeine, not really experiencing the last bit of love from our family. Before we see May, I will. I'm going to sleep. I will be there for her, completely.

"I love us," I say, feeling the loss of sleep. It takes me out of my turn and time. It takes me out of time. Whose adventure was I on?

42

I SIT DOWN ON THE log and get ready to tell them all about it.

"I am not getting it," says Gary.

"She hasn't explained it yet," Hudson says back to him. Another fire, another peanut butter banana sandwich. With bottled water.

"Shhh, she's thinking of starting," says Tamra.

It's lunch time and they want to know why I think the way of a pioneer is paradoxical. This trip seems to have proven it to me on some level I have to share with the others, especially before May. Like, why are we still going? It seems like the closer we get to her, the less we have to bring out and make peace with. Because there will be none where she's been buried.

"Every generation is pushed to surpass the one that came before it. To pioneer new ideas, ways. The problems each generation faces are generally similar, and yet we like to think we are different. Pioneers are a futile breed. A soul worn-out on everything it has known and experienced, that will sacrifice all comfort for the feeling of adventure at any cost. We feel like we, now, know more about the world than we did, and we can actually conceive in our minds a state of knowing that the future will produce an even greater state of knowing. In reality, whatever knowledge we gain is simply replacing what we thought we knew as knowledge before. It was as valid, before it was demonstrated to be incorrect. And some things we replaced shouldn't have been replaced.

"Humanity did not gain a mastery over nature to destroy it. So we've civilized and secured parts of the world, made them our own. But we are still at the universe's mercy, all while behaving in arrogance to our only source of life. So many people have traveled the country or the world now, you've heard about it and you do it yourself and there are so many books about how going through this profound journey changes people or sets them apart from the others who didn't. You live vicariously through that initially. And it's like the only possible way to have a genuine experience is to do something new. You guys remember that guy on YouTube who ate one-hundred fifty Warheads? Some other guy will end up doing two-hundred. Everybody strives to invent something new to contribute to the human race. But some of those contributions are foolish, a waste of time. And it's weird, because we feel the need to secede from what's come before. We think our way is going to be easier, but there is an intensive trial to determine that. So like explorers we set out to thrive in new environments and under different teachings. And it comes at a cost. I remember one of my classmates flipping through the Multi-variable Calculus textbook and he was disgusted with the methods. He was convinced that there was a better way. So he could go and try and find them, or write a better book to teach people how to learn Calculus, and that happens all the time. Everyone's ideas are challenged, but I really think it's more just to validate ourselves by identifying someone else's tiny errors. So we venture out to find these brave new worlds or unfounded lifestyles in the society that, although they don't understand us, did the same exact thing when they were growing up. It causes us to suffer, to question and value these abnormal beliefs. But those beliefs aren't true.

"What happened to the Puritans once they got settled in the Americas? They ended up persecuting the Quakers in a very similar fashion that the Catholics persecuted them. They escaped all this horror, and cross the ocean, face death and pestilence, only to inevitably bring that death with them and wipe out what was there before, the Native Americans. As we ourselves yearn for this new experience, we realize that people have been traveling south to north for centuries, going for food or for something to do. We have the motivation of May, but we're pioneers in our own way, with this relationship, you know? But I can't say a polyamorous relationship is better. I don't even know the difference. I just do know that certain pioneers are off in their thinking when they invest time into just any discovery. There's a doubt cast over the self then, indicative of that point."

Everyone is silent. I meander a little bit after that, but it becomes an open forum. We all try to wrap our heads around what I just said. Tamra doesn't buy it, but she enjoys debating for argument's sake. I don't know what it means, really. I just want to tell them my thoughts so maybe they will share theirs with mine.

43

"I LOVE US," I SAY, snapping my body in place rigidly. My glasses seem to make the blurs in my vision more intoxicating as focus is out of the question, so I close my eyes. We're not stopping anymore. There's enough gas in the tank to get to May. "How much time has passed?" I ask Gary. I open my eyes.

"About two hours since you closed you eyes."

This is the final lap. We're exhausted, reckless, letting Tamra drive the rest of the way as she is coming down from her high. "It's a bit like May always said. It doesn't matter how fucked-up you get if you already know the truth."

She's speeding and normally I would say something to put her in her place in order to get her to slow down, but instead I give my attention the land flashing by. "We're like a band. Are we broken up?" I ask.

"Like a band?" Hudson asks.

"No. Like our relationship. Are we still together? I never figured it out."

"Do you want to be?" Gary asks.

"No, no, don't put it on her," Hudson says. "She's not in the greatest shape."

"That's how we all feel, Hudson," Tamra says.

"Guys, guys," I say. "Love." The sun peeks through the clouds. There was a downpour earlier. It was our last stop, to get soaking wet and wring some of the grime out of our clothes and skin. When the sun goes down, it'll be dark. It's in the dark that we'll see May, and we'll probably stay there all night, until the sun comes up again. And decisions will be made. Returning the rental car, life resuming with or without one and other.

I believe I've had enough, but I don't know where they stand. I could imagine Tamra and Hudson banding together, but even more likely would be Gary and Tamra, them shutting Hudson out and inviting me along. Or Tamra coming to only me, like Hudson did to May. There's no telling with these people sometimes. Though I pass out again, I drift in and out. At one point I hear them.

"I haven't kept in touch with Ana, but I could have met you guys in New Orleans and that's why I didn't," Hudson says.

"What the hell? Why not? Ana misses you," Tamra says.

"There's one thing I wanted to ask her, that I always wondered about."

"What is that?" Gary asks.

"Well, she always likened her job at Barter's like an abusive relationship. When she stormed out that day, I heard she wouldn't come back. And I was happy for her. She deserved more than what that place gave to her."

"But—"

"Why'd she go back? Then I think of May. Because, she didn't think we were all abusive, did she?"

44

TAMRA PULLS UP ON THE curb adjacent to a big building that's fenced in. We exit the Camry and cross the street. Hudson is the first to jump over the road blocker that keeps cars from driving into the cemetery at night. It is going to take a lot longer to find her without the car, but we don't want to wait until morning now that we are here. Hopefully there isn't any security.

Tamra and Gary pass me into Hudson's arms on the other side of the barrier and then jump over by themselves. The cemetery is enclosed by a wall of stones so we feel okay turning on our flashlight. May's family had at least given us the information of where she was buried, which we're hoping wasn't a lie.

We walk then stop at a pond that casts a powerful reflection of tonight's half-moon, not all there but bright as can be. We each see each other and sit down for a moment.

"You wanted to know if we are together, Bunny?" Hudson asks. "I think we are."

"Sure," says Gary. He looks over to Tamra. "Hey, how far into the future could we make it without May?"

"Enough questions, I need to think," Tamra says.

"Okay."

"There's something else I've been wondering about," I say.

"Shoot," says Hudson.

"All those times May said but fuck it, did she mean but fuck it like fuck it or butt-fuck it?"

"I have no idea."

"Really?" Tamra asks.

"I would think she meant butt-fuck it," says Gary. "She *enjoyed* anal."

"Mhm," I say. "I remember."

Tamra rose up from the ground, anxiously shuffling along in tandem with wiping the dirt off of her behind as the slope back to the graves held her up. "You coming though?"

Sometime later after checking countless other tombstones in the area we find Helen Linnaeus, May's mother. Her grave is adorned with flowers, and her tombstone carved after some skyscraper and we debate which one it could be. To the right of Helen is May. This is what we were afraid of.

May's grave wasn't as well-planned out as her mother's. With the knowledge that she would die, Helen made a tombstone in advance. May had no plans for her grave. We also like to think she had no plans for dying, but you never know.

"Just what the fuck happened?" Tamra asks, laying down over May's grave. I realize she wasn't talking to us now. "We knew it, that maybe you wanted to die. But we also knew you didn't want to be buried next to this miserable cunt!"

The story— something we'd only heard from unreliable sources— was that May had taken care of her mother in her final dying days, but before Helen died May went first. They found both of the bodies in Helen's house that she liked to keep stuffy and messy. May's was sprawled out on the couch, her face slumped against the floor. Helen was in her bed with what they concluded was a self-inflicted neck wound. She'd slit her throat. We thought May had done it but May had been dead a few days longer than Helen.

We can only speculate how it had happened, especially after May's last text. The text that had brought us here:

If if yu can make it, don't.

So just like she did with her mother, or so we interpret it, we gathered the family together to figure this out. Until her family contacted Tamra about what had happened. We have nothing more to go off of than that. The best we can do is pretend to ourselves that at the end of the line, we'll find her again. Each of us, even me who wasn't really involved, feels this insult. We had planned on exhuming her and relocating the grave site, but now that we're actually here we think better of it.

"May's family must not know this was against her wishes?" Gary says.

"I bet they're just completely obviously," Tamra says through a scowl.

"We have to do something," Hudson points out.

"Hudson is right," Gary adds.

"We have to do something for ourselves," says Tamra. "We have to live on for May. We're barely getting by. We sacrificed all we had before just to get here. Now here we are, let's say goodbye to her and do her the solid of letting it be."

"She's resting in peace because there's no afterlife," I say. "I can only imagine what a horror awareness of eternity is."

"You're saying because she can't feel being buried next to her mother, it's okay?" Hudson asks, mouth wide open.

"More along the lines of, what are we suppose to do, Hudson?" Gary asks him, patting him on the shoulder.

"Like I said, we forge ahead," says Tamra.

"Pioneers or not," I add.

We sit with each other for the next few hours and hate ourselves for not making it in time for the funeral or not being able to act in such a way that would have kept May safe in Denver. Even if she was miserable there, it was better than dead, right? May might not be watching us, but we're so young and still have a powerful imagination. We're not just one.

"I love us," I say. If May's spirit did make itself known, she would come to us, a girl in a suit with twinkling blue flats but no legs. With hands but empty sleeves. No face, but it would be May's figure. Slowly because the gravity would not affect her metaphysical presence, she would bring herself down and dance with the wind among her living loves.

Each of us gets a turn, if we want one.

Thank you SO MUCH for reading this book!!!

If you enjoyed it, I do hope you'll leave a review from wherever you bought it, or at Goodreads. As an indie author, I cannot understate the importance of reviews. They pretty much determine whether or not I can continue producing more lovely content and get it out to you in an orderly fashion. On top of that, they allow me to improve the way I do things and thus create even greater stories. If you're interested in receiving a free review copy of any of my other titles, leave an honest review for this book where you purchased it. Send a link of your review to rsreverie@gmail.com. I'll smile, and send the next book of your choice right over!

I have a lot of interesting stuff coming soon (I'm still tinkering with a short story from May's perspective for instance). Why, you should see me working on all the books I'm working on. Sadly, that could turn weird. So instead, I'll tell you that if you'd like to know more about what's next on my end, you should join my mailing list at:

http://www.starbloak.com

When you sign-up, I also send you a free ebook copy my comic fantasy book *First Reality*. And that's just the beginning for my wonderful readers. I share updates for upcoming projects, discounts, and interesting tidbits I come across in my journey to being a real boy.

My Books

Swiftopia- a dystopian satire where Taylor Swift has taken the world by storm- literally. Imagine a zombie apocalypse, just replace the zombies with Taylor Swift fans.

First Reality- a comic fantasy novel that serves as a parody to video game RPG's and tired fantasies.

GOD & everything- a one-act comedy following GOD around, ensuring laughter and thought as well as calling out some of religion's more unscrupulous behavior.

Freckles Over Scars- a collection of short stories of varying genres all revolving around the same theme, the premise of healing and reconstruction.

These titles are available at:
www.starbloak.com/books.html

www.starbloak.com/video.html

So see that link above?

That will lead you to my Youtube channel.

More specifically, I produce content such as:

Fried Philosophy: thought discourse on philosophical topics. Explained in a accessible & entertaining fashion.

The Thought Program: Ever since 2008, I've been collecting peoples thoughts on index cards. This video series shares more of that story and the thoughts gathered over the years.

Music covers: Some of my favorite bands are Super Time Pilot, Meg & Dia, System Of A Down, Eve 6, Green Day, & The Mountain Goats

First Reality Podcast: A (mostly) biweekly podcast of the unabridged audiobook version of my comic fantasy/ parody *First Reality*.

& other assorted stuff I felt like doing last week! Please subscribe, you know, if you're into it.

About The Author

Ryan Starbloak is author to several books of varying genres, a Youtuber (having first appeared on the medium through Rob Potylo's *Quiet Desperation*), and musician from Lynn, Massachusetts. He currently lives in New Orleans, Louisiana.

Connect with Ryan on

Tumblr:
https://www.ryanstarbloak.tumblr.com

Facebook:
https://www.facebook.com/starbloak/

Email:
rsreverie@gmail.com